How Long Had It Been Since Marybeth Had Felt A Man's Body Against Her Own?

Too long, she decided as her fingers found the nape of Gunner's neck. He spun her, making her laugh, and she clung to him, dizzy with sensations that pulsed through her.

Much too soon the song ended, and he stopped moving. A good five seconds hummed between them before he released her. As they stepped apart, he kept her hand firmly in his. Confused, she sought his gaze . . . and found a new emotion in those brown eyes. Passion burned there, dark and haunting, pulling at her like nothing had ever pulled at her in her life.

"Thanks for the dance." His voice was husky and low.

She felt drawn toward him by something primitive and wild, totally out of her control. *This can't be happening,* her mind screamed. A man cannot make a woman feel this way with a simple look and touch.

But Gunner had.

Dear Reader,

Q. What does our heroine know about the hero when she first meets him?
A. Not much!

His personality, background, family—his entire life—is a total mystery. I started to think that the heroine never *truly* knows what's in store for her when she first sees the hero. In fact, *her* life from that moment on can be likened to an adventure with a "mysterious" man. And it's from these thoughts that our Valentine's Day promotion, MYSTERY MATES, was born. After all, who *is* this guy and what *is* he looking for?

Each of our heroes this month is a certain type of man, as I'm sure you can tell from the title of each February Desire book. The *Man of the Month* by Raye Morgan is *The Bachelor* . . . a man who never dreamed he'd have anything to do with—*children!* Cait London brings us *The Cowboy,* Ryanne Corey *The Stranger,* Beverly Barton *The Wanderer* and from Karen Leabo comes *The Cop.*

Peggy Moreland's hero, *The Rescuer,* is a very special man indeed. For while his story is completely fictitious, the photo on the cover is that of a Houston, Texas, fire fighter. Picked from a calendar the Houston Fire Department creates for charity, this man is truly a hero.

So, enjoy our MYSTERY MATES. They're sexy, they're handsome, they're lovable . . . and they're only from Silhouette Desire.

Lucia Macro
Senior Editor

PEGGY MORELAND

THE RESCUER

SILHOUETTE *Desire*
Published by Silhouette Books New York
America's Publisher of Contemporary Romance

For my Inie, who fills our lives with her love.

Special thanks:
. . . to Terrell, Texas, my hometown and
a wonderful place to grow up.
. . . and to Terence Lyon
for answering endless questions about firemen,
and for a friendship that goes back to first grade.
. . . and to Manuel Chavez, a fire fighter who takes his
dedication to his job above and beyond the call of duty.

SILHOUETTE BOOKS
300 East 42nd St., New York, N.Y. 10017

THE RESCUER

Copyright © 1993 by Peggy Bozeman Morse

ISBN: 0-373-05765-2

First Silhouette Books printing February 1993

All the characters in this book have no existence outside the
imagination of the author and have no relation whatsoever to
anyone bearing the same name or names. They are not even
distantly inspired by any individual known or unknown to the
author, and all incidents are pure invention.

Printed in the U.S.A.

Books by Peggy Moreland

Silhouette Desire

A Little Bit Country #515
Run for the Roses #598
Miss Prim #682
The Rescuer #765

PEGGY MORELAND,

a native Texan, has moved nine times in seventeen years of marriage. She has come to look at her husband's transfers as "extended vacations." Each relocation has required a change of career for Peggy: high school teacher, real-estate broker, accountant, antique-shop owner. Now the couple resides in Oklahoma with their three children, and Peggy is working on a master's degree in creative studies while doing what she loves best—writing!

A Letter from the Author

Dear Reader:

During my senior year in college, I was whining how I didn't have a date for the weekend, when a co-worker offered to "fix me up" with her husband's best friend, Frederick.

I hate blind dates and had suffered through my share, so I had no desire to be "fixed up" with anyone. But before I had a chance to weasel my way out of the situation, she was on the phone. As she dialled, she casually mentioned that Frederick loved horses and was a disabled Vietnam vet.

"Disabled?" I asked. "In what way?"

"He was shot in the head."

Shot in the head! Always one with a vivid imagination, I immediately envisioned opening my apartment door to greet the headless horseman ... or worse.

What I didn't realize at the time was that the blind date was only half-blind—and I was the blind half. Frederick's vision was 20/20. Before agreeing to go out with me, he and my co-worker's husband snuck into the building where I worked and checked me out through a strip of glass in my office door while I was engrossed in finding a seven-cent error in the scholarship fund.

After seventeen years of marriage, I think it's safe to assume he liked what he saw. And I did, too ... once I determined that his head was attached to his neck and not carried in his hand!

Sincerely,

Peggy Moreland

One

Sunbeams danced across Miranda's face, warming her cheek and tickling her eyelashes, gently nudging her away from her dreams. Like a kitten, she stretched, arching her back and inching her fingertips toward the brass headboard.

Without opening her eyes, she knew it was morning. And she didn't want it to be. Not yet. She curled into a tight ball and tried to recapture the threads of her dream. Such a nice dream, too. She'd been dancing, her hair swept up high on her head and diamonds glittering at her ears and at her throat. She'd been wearing the red dress, the sequined one that shimmered when the light hit it just right, as if it were woven with a million twinkling stars.

She squinched her eyes tightly against the intrusive sunlight and tried to conjure up the image of the man she'd been dancing with. He was handsome...

naturally. Miranda Morley would settle for nothing less. But she wanted to remember every feature.

Black hair, she recalled. Black as sin, Juanita would say. A little long on the neck, but not overly so, and thick with just a hint of curl. His eyes were dark. Black? No, brown, she remembered on a breathy sigh. Like warm, dark chocolate. When he had spun her around the dance floor, those brown eyes had been leveled on her... and every other woman in the room had been sick with envy.

Smiling, she dreamed on until the sun blurred his image behind her closed lids, dissipating it into thin wisps like a cloud on a windy day. A regretful sigh lifted her chest and warmed her pillow where her cheek rested. She hugged her arms around her chest, holding his memory close, remembering how he had held her, her breasts pressed tight— *Breasts*?

She jerked upright, the dream, for the moment, forgotten. Catching the neckline of her nightgown, she stretched it out and peeked inside.

Her shoulders slumped in despair. "Still no boobs," she said, and let the elastic snap back into place. And Juanita had promised. She had told Miranda that if she ate all her vegetables, drank all her milk, and said her rosaries like a good little girl she'd have boobs just like Juanita's in no time.

Her lips puckered in a pout, Miranda shoved back the comforter and climbed from the bed. She peeled off her nightgown, dropped it to the floor and stared at her reflection in the cheval mirror. Juanita had lied. She was still as flat as a pancake. And the night before she'd eaten all her broccoli, drank two full glasses of milk, said her rosaries and had even thrown in two Hail Mary's for good measure.

With a last woeful look, she turned her back on the disappointing image in the mirror and pulled her training bra from the dresser. She knew Marybeth had bought the bra just to humor her. She'd overheard her mother saying that very thing to Juanita. But Marybeth didn't understand how badly she wanted boobs.

And, oh, how Miranda wanted boobs! Big ones just like Juanita's. The kind that filled up a bra with enough left over to smile up at a person over the top. Not little ones like her mother's.

She frowned as she settled the bra over her eight-year-old chest. Unfortunately it seemed she had inherited her mother's figure.

Oh well, she reasoned as she stuffed wads of tissue into each cup. Things could be worse. She could have been born a boy. And that would have been horrible, because no one craved or appreciated femininity more than Miranda.

Crossing to her closet, she thumbed through the clothes hanging there, trying to decide what to wear. Nothing suited her mood. Marybeth had promised her a trip to Dallas. Lunch in Neiman Marcus' Tea Room followed by a day of shopping till she dropped. That scenario required a more mature look than anything *her* closet offered.

Picking up the threads of her dream once again—the red sequined dress and the man with hair as black as sin—she hummed, dragging a lazy finger down the wall's length as she strolled down the hall to her mother's room. The song she hummed was the one from her dream, the one they'd danced to—"Unforgettable," by Natalie and Nat King Cole—and Mir-

anda's absolute favorite song...for the moment. Her
taste in music, as her every other preference, fluctu-
ated daily.

At the master bedroom, she peeked around the
opened door and saw that her mother was still sleeping. Fully aware her mother had returned in the wee
hours of the morning from a business trip to San
Francisco, she tiptoed past the bed and across the
room to the dressing area beyond.

Her mother's dressing room was Miranda's most
favorite place in the entire house. She'd spent hours
there trying on and discarding outfits from her mother's closet and applying makeup with the skill of an
artist. There was no hesitation when she approached
this closet. She knew just which dress she wanted. She
slid back the mirrored doors and pulled out the black
sheath. Classy, sophisticated, and with the right belt,
wearable.

Without bothering to unzip it, she pulled the dress
over her head, then thumbed through the rack of belts
until she found a wide brass one. A few minor adjust-
ments and the belt was in place. Miranda then turned
to the vanity. A little eyeliner, a touch of blue shadow,
a flick or two of the mascara wand across her lashes
and she was ready for lipstick. *Flaming Passion,* she
decided, after studying the assortment in the drawer.
It suited her mood.

Completely dressed now, she turned a profile to the
mirror and filled her lungs with a deep breath. She
held it a moment while she admired her reflection. Her
breasts—or rather, her bra—poked out in all the right
places.

Satisfied with the results, she smiled as she went to
wake Marybeth.

"Marybeth?" she whispered at her mother's side. When her mother didn't move, she touched a hand to her shoulder and shook. "Marybeth," she repeated in a louder voice. "Wake up." Marybeth didn't so much as flinch a muscle. Miranda shook harder. Hard enough that Marybeth rolled to her back. But her eyes remained stubbornly closed.

Leaning closer, Miranda pushed up one eyelid with the tip of her index finger and waited, half expecting her mother to scream "Boo!" at any second and tug Miranda onto the bed for a tickle. But Marybeth didn't move.

Something wasn't right, Miranda concluded. Saturday mornings were *their* time, Marybeth's and Miranda's, and Marybeth always looked as forward to that time as Miranda. Could she be sick? No, Miranda dispelled that thought with a decisive shake of her head. Marybeth was never sick, but just to be sure she inched a little closer to peer at her mother's unblinking eye. The white of the exposed eye was laced with teensy red lines, and the circle of blue within was dull and sightless.

Miranda jerked back her hand and suppressed a shudder. If Marybeth was playing a game, Miranda didn't like it one bit. But maybe it wasn't a game, her overactive and decidedly dramatic mind reasoned. Maybe...

She reached for the phone. The child of a single parent, she'd heard the emergency lecture often enough to know just what to do. And since they'd moved from their condo in Dallas to the house in Terrell, she'd heard the lecture at least a hundred more times.

Picking up the phone, she calmly dialed 9-1-1. "This is Miranda Morley," she told the dispatcher who answered. "My address is 407 Maple Drive. I think my mother is dead."

Marybeth awakened to the sound of splintering wood, but it was the scream of the alarm that had her rocketing from the bed. Disoriented, she stood with her palms flattened against her ears and tried to remember the emergency escape for the hotel in which she was staying. She staggered to the door, squinting eyes that felt as if they'd been polished with coarse sandpaper, and groped blindly for the escape route she knew was posted there.

But I'm not in a hotel, her befuddled mind reasoned when her fingertips found only smooth wood. Forcing her eyes to focus, she glanced back at the bed. That was *her* peach comforter on the bed, those were *her* suitcases piled at its foot, and obviously that was *her* alarm that was threatening to deafen her.

But which alarm? While she had been in San Francisco, her mother had insisted on having both a burglar and a fire alarm installed. Marybeth had never heard either of the alarms in action and hadn't a clue which one was blaring or for that matter how to shut the damn thing off!

But Miranda did. Miranda had told her over the phone about watching the man install it and being the one allowed to test the system.

Marybeth's hands slipped from her ears to her mouth. "Oh, dear God," she whispered against trembling fingers. "Miranda."

Jerking open the bedroom door, she stumbled down the hall, her head pounding a cadence in perfect symphony with the shrill pulsations of the alarm. Her hands found their way back to her ears, but her thoughts remained fixed on reaching Miranda. She inhaled deeply as she ran, searching for the telltale scent of smoke, but detected only a hint of gardenias, Miranda's latest choice in perfume.

"Miranda!" she screamed, knowing even as she did that her voice couldn't be heard over the alarm's piercing siren. At her daughter's door, she stopped, her chest heaving beneath a faded T-shirt, her fingernails digging into the door frame. But the bed was empty. Miranda was nowhere in sight.

A wad of fear rose in her throat. Kidnapped. Hadn't her mother fretted over that very possibility? Wasn't that the very reason she'd insisted Marybeth have such a sophisticated burglar alarm system installed? *There are crazies in this world,* her mother had warned, *who wouldn't think twice about snatching a child as beautiful and precocious as Miranda. Especially if they thought there might be some ransom money to be made off the deal.*

Fighting back tears, Marybeth pushed herself away from the doorway and ran. *Oh, dear God,* she prayed as she rounded the corner, *please let Miranda be safe.* Blinded by tears, she didn't see the dark wall of humanity until she'd slammed dead into it. Before she could react, arms, thick and powerful, encircled her, capturing her in a steellike vise. Instinct had her clawing and fighting to free herself, but the arms tightened, lifting her off her feet.

"Let me go!" she screamed as she pummeled the man's chest and face with her fists. "What have you done with Miranda?"

There was a grunt when her foot connected with the man's shin and for a split second his grip on her went slack. Her toes touched the floor and Marybeth used that added impetus to shove hard against his chest. Free, she ducked around him, but before she could make good her escape, she was up against the wall, her hands pinned above her head, his body flat against hers. His face was shoved to within inches of hers. For the first time Marybeth had a good look at her captor. She swallowed hard against the fear that rose in her throat while the alarm speaker suspended on the wall above her head threatened to deafen her.

If looks could kill, she knew she'd already be dead. The eyes that met hers were dark and piercing . . . and one of them had already begun to swell. A blue vessel at his temple protruded, throbbing an angry accompaniment to the twitch of the muscle on his left jaw. The hands that held her wrists against the wall would easily make two of hers. And his chest . . . Lord, his chest. Solid as a brick wall. She closed her eyes against the reality of her chances of overpowering this man.

Marybeth stilled her struggles, but every muscle in her body remained rigid and ready for any chance of escape. "Do whatever you want with me," she said, lifting her chin in defiance, "but if you so much as harm a hair on my daughter's head, I'll kill you."

His cheek grazed hers, a night's growth of beard scraping against her smooth skin as he forced his face to hers. Marybeth recoiled as his breath heaved hot and invasive at her ear.

"Lady," he said, his voice low and threatening, "I'm not here to hurt you *or* your daughter. I'm a fireman answering a call. Now where's the victim?"

It took a moment for the man's words to sink in, but when they did, Marybeth's muscles turned to noodle consistency. "Victim?" she echoed weakly.

"Yes, victim," he said, his voice tight with irritation. "Now where—"

The alarm stopped, startling the man into silence.

"Miranda," Marybeth whispered as relief washed over her in waves. She wrenched her hands from the man's grasp and shot down the hall toward the kitchen. She pushed through the swinging door and then stopped, her trembling fingers once again finding their way to her lips as she watched Miranda climb down from the bar stool she'd pushed beneath the alarm's control panel.

After slipping her feet into a pair of her mother's high heels, Miranda turned and when she saw Marybeth a smile bloomed on her face. "Hi, Marybeth. Did you hear the alarm?"

Marybeth nearly wept. "Yes," she managed to say as she dropped to her knees and opened her arms. "I heard the alarm, darling."

Miranda stepped into the embrace. Marybeth rocked to and fro, squeezing Miranda as if she'd never let her go. "Honey, are you okay?" she asked, fighting back tears.

"I'm fine, Marybeth."

"Then why did you set off the alarm?"

Laughing, Miranda wriggled, inching backward until she could see her mother's face. "I didn't, but I can't wait to tell Mamere how good it works. She—" Her gaze drifted from her mother to a point above and beyond her. Her smile melted and her expression turned moonstruck. "It's him," she whispered breathlessly.

Him? Him, who? Puzzled, Marybeth turned to find the fireman standing behind her. He looked no less threatening than he had when he'd held her pinned to the wall. Slowly she rose to her feet, placing herself protectively between Miranda and his threatening presence.

"I'm s-s-sorry," she stammered nervously. "It seems there's been some kind of mista—"

"Is there an emergency here or not?" the fireman demanded impatiently.

Marybeth tugged at the hem of her T-shirt in an attempt to lengthen it. "Well—" she began. "I don't think so."

"Do you realize there's a stiff fine for alerting the 9-1-1 service without cause?"

Marybeth pushed her fingertips at her temples as the man's voice rose in volume. Even under normal circumstances, she wasn't her best at 7:00 a.m. on a Saturday morning. And these circumstances were anything but normal. "I realize that," she said, struggling for patience. "But I didn't call 9-1-1."

"Well, who did?" he demanded angrily.

Marybeth's temper flared to match his. "If you'd quit firing questions at me for a minute, I might be able to get to the bottom—"

"Marybeth didn't call," Miranda said as she slipped around her mother to stand in front of the fireman. "I did."

The second Miranda stepped into view, the man's expression went from narrow-eyed, tight-lipped fury to wide-eyed, slack-mouthed disbelief. Marybeth didn't have to wonder about the sudden change in his expression. She may have been upset when she first burst into the kitchen, but she wasn't blind.

Make-up two inches thick, a black sheath dress and stiletto heels were hard to ignore when worn by an eight-year-old. She was accustomed to her daughter's little idiosyncrasies...unfortunately, others weren't. And at the moment she wasn't in the mood to try to explain Miranda's sense of fashion to anyone, least of all this irate fireman. She had a crisis to deal with.

"All right, young lady," she said in her firmest I-mean-business voice. "Why did you call 9-1-1?"

Tears welled in Miranda's eyes and her lower lip began to quiver. "But you told me to," she wailed.

Marybeth's mouth dropped open, but before she could deny her participation in this fiasco, the fireman was nudging her aside.

"Why don't I ask the questions," he said, snatching away, no matter how subtly, whatever control Marybeth had over the situation. He hunkered down in front of Miranda and offered her a lop-sided grin. The tears miraculously disappeared from the child's eyes. "What's your name, honey?" he asked gently.

"Miranda Morley." She returned his smile and stepped a little closer, tottering slightly in her mother's high heels. "What's yours?"

"Gunner Keith."

"Are you a fireman?"

"Yes."

"Do you like to dance?"

Before he could respond to Miranda's last outrageous question, a second fireman stuck his head around the kitchen's swinging door. The man glanced quickly around, his gaze settling on Marybeth's bare legs. Wishing she'd chosen something a little less revealing as sleepwear, she once again tugged the hem of her T-shirt a little farther down her thigh.

He shifted his gaze upward until his eyes met hers. He smiled a wolfish smile. Though his words were directed at Gunner, his gaze remained fixed on Marybeth. "The ambulance and the police are here."

Without sparing the man a glance, Gunner took Miranda's hand in his. "Send 'em home, Joe," he said gruffly, then more softly to Miranda, "And yes, I like to dance."

"Me, too," she said on a breathy sigh.

The second fireman's eyes bugged open as he listened to the exchange. He opened his mouth as if he might say something, then closed it and shrugged. He left the kitchen, chuckling.

Gunner stood but kept Miranda's hand in his. "Maybe sometime when I'm not on duty, I'll check you out and see how light you are on your feet." He smiled an apology. "But right now I've got to file a report. Do you mind answering a few questions for me?"

Miranda fairly beamed. "No, I don't mind."

"Good." Gunner took a pad from his pocket and flipped it open. "Did you call in at 6:43 this morning and report that your mother was dead?"

On hearing this bit of news, Marybeth's mouth sagged open wide enough to catch flies, but Miranda didn't bat an eye. Her lips puckered prettily beneath the smear of bright red lipstick before she replied. "I believe I said I *thought* she was dead."

Marybeth closed her mouth on a groan.

Gunner shifted his gaze from Miranda to Marybeth. The look he shot her was damning.

"And this woman is your mother?"

The way he said *this woman* set Marybeth's teeth on edge.

Miranda glanced over her shoulder at Marybeth then turned her full attention back to the fireman. "Yes," she replied with the certainty a prosecuting attorney would kill for if it came from a corroborating witness.

"So she's not dead nor in any life-threatening situation?"

"No," Miranda replied slowly, then smiled. "But I thought she was. When I tried to wake her she didn't move and when I pushed up her eyelids, her eyes looked dead."

Gunner glanced again at Marybeth. If possible, his scowl darkened perceptibly. And that made Marybeth mad. Damn mad. Granted, Miranda's description of the morning's happenings was not placing Marybeth in a very favorable light, but how dare this man look at her as if she were some kind of irresponsible mother.

In an attempt to regain control of the situation, Marybeth held on to the threads of her temper and offered politely, "As you can see, I'm not dead or suffering any medical emergency." The absurdity of the entire morning's events suddenly hit her and she clapped a hand over her mouth to smother a laugh. "Although when you had me pinned against the wall in the hall, I did fear a heart attack."

The scowl remained fixed on his face. Obviously the man had been born minus a sense of humor.

She decided to try diplomacy. "Look," she said, once again placing herself between Miranda and the fireman. "I'm afraid this is all my fault. You see, being a single parent, I've taught Miranda all the emergency numbers and instructed her to use them if ever I were incapacitated." When he continued to frown at her, she gave up on diplomacy and decided on force. She caught him by the elbow and before he could argue the point had hustled him through the kitchen's swinging door. "I'm sorry for any inconvenience we've caused you and I thank you for your quick response to Miranda's call. Being new to the area, it's comforting to know we can depend on—"

Her hand went slack on his arm. Splintered wood lay scattered across the entry hall floor at her feet. The dead bolt, once securely moored in the thick oak door, looked like so much twisted metal. Although the front door itself was intact, the frame surrounding it was destroyed.

"What happened?" she breathed in a hoarse whisper.

Gunner gave the door a cursory glance before stooping to scoop his hat from the floor. "When we don't receive a response, it's our policy to forcibly enter a residence." He was halfway through the doorway when Marybeth grabbed again at his arm.

"Wait a minute!" she said, her voice rising hysterically. "You can't leave yet! What about the door?"

"The door?" he repeated, frowning and looking back at the object in question. "If you've got some nails we can board it up."

"I don't want my front door boarded up!"

He shrugged a whatever-you-say shrug. "My responsibility is to see that the residence is secure."

"Then whose responsibility is it to repair it?" she demanded.

"The homeowner's."

"But I don't know how to repair a door!"

"Check the Yellow Pages. Carpenters are listed under the Cs." He dropped the fireman's hat onto his head, tapped the brim in salute, then turned and walked away.

Marybeth stood in the doorway and stared after him too stunned to move.

Out of nowhere, Miranda appeared and melted against her mother's side. "Marybeth?" she asked in a small and trembly voice. "If we can't lock our door, will the boogeyman get us?"

During his ten-year stint with the fire department, Gunner Keith had responded to all sorts of emergencies. Some real, some only imagined. None, he decided, quite matched up to his experience on this particular call.

By all rights, he shouldn't even have been there. He was on the last leg of a twenty-four-hour shift when the call had come in. He could have walked out the door and gone home and let the next shift respond. He could have. But he hadn't.

And now he had it to deal with.

He slammed the truck door in an attempt to shut out the echoes of fear he'd heard in the little girl's voice. It didn't work. *Will the boogeyman get us?* Nerves frayed from a sleepless night and too much coffee stretched a little tighter.

"Kind of hard on the lady, weren't you, Chief?"

Gunner gritted his teeth to keep from biting off his driver's head.

"'If you've you got some nails...'" Joe shook his head in disbelief. "I can't believe you said that to her."

Gunner shot his partner a look that had the reputation for sending most of the men in the firehouse running for cover. As usual, Joe ignored it.

"Gunner, you know damn good and well we're supposed to secure a residence we've forced. And that means more than boarding up the front door."

Gunner's shoulder rose and fell in a so-what shrug. "She doesn't know that."

"Yeah, but you do."

Gunner inched down in the seat, tipping his hat to shade his overtired eyes from the morning sun's glare. "I assure you, I won't lose any sleep over it."

"Like hell," Joe said under his breath.

Gunner heard the remark and frowned. A cold-hearted son of a bitch. That was what everyone at the station called him . . . with the exception of Joe. Why Joe thought differently was beyond him, for Gunner had never done anything to change that image. Rather than argue the point as to whether he'd lose sleep over the Morley's problem or not, he kept his mouth shut, hoping Joe would do the same.

He didn't.

"She was a looker, wasn't she?"

Joe drove like he talked. Fast. Gunner's foot pumped the floorboard, working an imaginary brake. "Who?"

"The kid's mother."

Gunner looked at Joe in surprise. His partner's reputation around the station was that of a ladies' man, but at the moment Gunner wondered if Joe needed his vision checked. The woman *he'd* dealt with was a frigging mess. Hair that looked like maybe she'd stuck a finger in an electrical socket then tried to calm it down with glue. A raggedy T-shirt any teenager with a modicum of pride would have been ashamed to be seen in and enough red lines in her eyes to illustrate ten road maps. "If you care for drunks," he said, bracing a knee against the dash as Joe careened around a corner.

"Drunk! That lady wasn't drunk."

"Hung over, then. You'd have to be blind to miss the signs."

"Then I must be blind. Enlighten me."

"So dead asleep the kid couldn't wake her. Blood-shot eyes. Sensitivity to noise."

Joe rolled his eyes. "For God's sake. If somebody beat your door down at the crack of dawn on a Saturday morning, even *you* might not appear at your best."

Gunner might have taken offense if he'd heard the sarcasm in Joe's remark. But he hadn't heard. His conscience was playing havoc with his attention span. "There ought to be a law," he said, and automatically braced his shoulder against the door when Joe swerved around a car ahead of them.

"About what?"

"Mothers," Gunner said in disgust. "Did you see that kid? Dressed like a whore at 7:00 a.m. on a Saturday morning. Obviously the poor little thing doesn't get much guidance or supervision. There ought to be a law," he repeated in disgust.

Joe chuckled and stole a glance at Gunner. "Bugging you, isn't it?"

The imaginary brake beneath Gunner's foot received a few more nervous pumps as the fire station came into view. "The only thing that bugs me is your driving skills," he said dryly.

Joe braked the truck to a neck-whipping stop inches from the fire station's brick exterior. "Like hell," he said, and pushed open his door. "You going back over there?"

Gunner shoved back his hat and wiped the nervous perspiration from his brow. He didn't know which was worse. Joe's driving or his busybody harping.

"The fire department's responsibility to the Morleys is complete," Gunner said as he climbed from the truck. He stretched the kinks out of his back, already thinking about his bed. "And not that it's any of your business," he added as he headed for the door of the station, "but I'm going to the feed store and pick up some feed." He slapped Joe on the back as he passed him. "Then I'm going home and sleep about twenty-four hours straight. I'd advise you to do the same."

Two

___

And that was exactly what Gunner did. He went to the feed store, loaded the back of his truck with fifty-pound bags of oats, climbed back in and headed for home, just as he'd told Joe he'd planned. It was on the way home that all his good intentions paved a few new streets in hell.

The trouble started with a glance at the sky. Weather was always a concern to Gunner, both as a fireman and as a rancher. The summer had been a particularly dry one. Grass fires were a nuisance that would soon turn to a major problem for the fire department if it didn't rain soon. Ponds were drying up all around the county, a constant cause of worry for the farmers and ranchers in the area.

As a fireman, he prayed daily for the sky to open up and bring rain, to dampen the soil and turn the grass green again. As a rancher, he added a second prayer that it would be a gentle rain, not a torrential down-pour that would flood the creeks and drown his cows or bring hail that would beat his last hay crop to a pulp.

But his glance at the sky showed only blue. Clear, crisp, lake water blue...

The same shade of blue as Marybeth Morley's underwear.

And that's where the trouble started.

At first his mind just sort of trailed off, blanking out the sky and the weather and focusing on only that peek of blue silk he'd glimpsed just below her T-shirt. Then it drifted further to recall the long stretch of tanned, bare thigh beneath.

Then he remembered other things. Things that at the time he hadn't been aware he'd even noticed. Like how tiny her feet were and the bright pink polish that covered the tips of her toes. How she'd stepped between him and the little girl ready to battle like a lioness protecting her cub. And the way her eyes had sparked in defense when he'd asked the kid if Marybeth was her mother.

He chuckled, remembering Miranda. Feisty little thing, that one. Stepping right up to him without a bit of fear to tell him she was the one who'd dialed 9-1-1. *Do you like to dance?* He laughed out loud, remembering. What a question! But then kids usually said the first thing that came to mind. He liked that innocence, that openness, that spit-in-your-eye, take-the-world-by-its-tail boldness unique to the young. They weren't tarnished by the ways of the world yet. They didn't know how to lie or charm.

Will the boogeyman get us? Gunner's smile dipped to a frown as the child's words came to mind again.

Troubled by his thoughts, he straightened behind the wheel, trying to ease the stab of guilt. He concentrated hard on the road and the chores that awaited him before he could finally go to bed...but he couldn't shake the sound of fear he'd heard in her voice.

"Damn that woman," he muttered under his breath. Setting his jaw, he slammed on the brakes and gave the wheel a hard jerk to the left. In the blink of an eye, the truck was headed in the opposite direction, back toward town, back toward 407 Maple Drive. Back toward the Morley residence.

"I'll fix the damn door and then I'm through," he told himself.

By the time he pulled up in front of the Morley home, he almost had himself believing it.

Heat prickled her skin, making an already short temper shorter by degrees. "I'm a grown woman," Marybeth muttered under her breath. "I can read directions, I can *follow* directions. I can even—" The screwdriver she wielded on the twisted lock slipped in her damp palm and she stumbled forward, slamming her head against the door.

In frustration she sank to the porch, rubbing a weary hand against her forehead. This wasn't turning out to be a very good day, a very good day at all. It had all started with the early morning visit from the fire department and had gone downhill ever since.

Miranda had sulked around all morning because their trip to Dallas had been canceled. She'd finally found a smile when Timmy, the little boy down the street, had come over to play.

Marybeth had barely recovered from that crisis when a new one presented itself. The man she'd found to repair the door had rebuilt the frame then skipped out on her while she'd gone to buy a new lock. She had a door, but she still couldn't lock it.

"I solved my other problems and I'll figure this one out, too." Unskilled but determined, she picked up the instruction sheet, which fluttered in the energy-sapping breeze, and frowned at it. "Okay," she murmured as she studied the diagrams. "If you follow steps one through twelve to install the dang thing, then it would make sense to simply start with twelve and go backward to un-install it."

With the instructions in one hand, she grabbed the screwdriver in the other and stood. She glanced at the twisted metal, then at the diagram of the finished project. She turned the piece of paper this way and that, trying to make the picture the same angle as her lock.

"Why me?" she groaned, and tossed the piece of paper over her shoulder.

Firming her lips, she jabbed the screwdriver in the twisted metal and began to tug. Afternoon sun sliced across the front porch, drawing beads of perspiration on her skin. An irritating rivulet of moisture worked its way down between her breasts.

A shadow fell across her hands, obstructing her view. A six-foot-two shadow to be exact. Slowly she turned her head and met the gaze of the fireman, the man who was the cause of all her problems in the first place.

His uniform was gone. He now wore jeans and a T-shirt. A ball cap had replaced the fireman's hat, but that same coal-black hair curled beneath the brim and at his neck. Swallowing a nasty remark, she turned her back to him and gave the lock a frustrated yank.

"If you'd unscrew the screws first, it ought to pop right out."

Perspiration stung her eyes and her hands ached from all the tugging she'd been doing. And the man's comment was irritating as hell. Did he take her for a fool? She'd already tried to unscrew the screws. They wouldn't budge so much as a centimeter. Curling her lip in disgust at both the man and his advice, she showed him her back once again. With her hip braced against the door for added leverage, she tried again. She tugged and tugged, grunted and groaned, but the lock still wouldn't budge.

"Here, let me try," he offered quietly.

The second his hand touched hers, Marybeth jerked back, her fingers scraping along the rough-edged metal. "Now look what you've done," she cried as she grabbed her index finger with her opposite hand.

"Let me see."

She popped her finger into her mouth, and shook her head, spinning away from him. "Just leave me alone," she mumbled around the injured appendage.

His hand caught her wrist and forced her to face him. "I'm a trained paramedic. Let me take a look."

Marybeth didn't want his help. She didn't like the man's attitude, but more, she didn't like the way her pulse kicked at his touch.

He forced her fingers open from the tight fist she had squeezed them into and bent his head over her hand. She held her breath as his fingers gently prodded hers. His hands were strong, his touch gentle, almost a caress. Nothing could have surprised her more. Heat crawled up her neck and warmed her cheeks. She assured herself it was a result of the sun that was searing a hole in her back.

"I don't see anything but a little scratch," he said, glancing up to meet her gaze.

His eyes were brown, lighter than she remembered, and softer than when he'd held her pinned against the wall. Then they'd been dark, full of anger and as frightening as her worst nightmare. His left eye was slightly swollen and tinged with red. Had she done that?

Her breath came out in a ragged whoosh. "It's my nail, you goose," she said to disguise her discomfort. She jerked her hand free. "You made me break my fingernail past the quick."

"Sorry."

She caught the glimmer of amusement in his eyes and glared at him. "Well, if you think you're so smart, you fix the damn thing!" She slapped the screwdriver into his hand then plopped down on the porch to nurse her wound.

Out of the corner of her eye she watched him move to hunker down in front of the door. He studied it a moment, then waved the screwdriver in the direction of the unpainted facing. "Who did that?"

"Mr. Peters. I found his name under the Cs," she said pointedly, reminding Gunner of his earlier advice. Then she frowned. "I should have looked under the Ds."

He paused in his work and looked at her, a brow lifted in question.

"For dependable," she explained. "While Miranda and I were at the hardware store picking up the new lock, Mr. Peters skipped out."

He shook his head and reapplied the screwdriver. "Never pay for a job until the work's complete."

Marybeth looked up at him in surprise. "How'd you know I paid him in advance?"

"I know Pete. He wouldn't have left without his money. Works long enough to earn the price of a bottle. He's probably half drunk by now."

"You might have warned me."

He shrugged. "Didn't ask."

While he talked, his hands worked the screwdriver. Muscles bunched beneath the short sleeves of his T-shirt with each sure twist of his hand. The strength behind the muscles was obvious as one by one the screws dropped to the porch. A last tug and the mangled lock popped free.

He stretched out a hand. "Pass me the new one."

Marybeth all but curled her lip. "I think that's disgusting."

"What?"

"I've been working on that stupid lock for over an hour," she said irritably as she pulled the new lock from its box. "And in two minutes, you're done. Disgusting," she repeated, and slapped the new piece of brass into his hand.

Their eyes met over the gleam of metal and clashed. She held one end of the polished brass, he held the other. Neither moved. The color of his eyes changed again, darkening with anger. They seemed to dare her to say something, anything, to give him an excuse to walk away.

Why was he so angry? she wondered irritably. She knew why *she* was in a bad mood. The man had broken her door and started a chain of events that had all but ruined her day.

But at least he'd had the decency to come back and repair it, she reminded herself.

Sighing, she dropped her hand. "I'm sorry for being so rude, but it's been a lousy day."

Without a word, Gunner turned to fit the new latch assembly in place. He didn't want her apology, he told himself as he pushed in a screw. He just wanted to fix the door and go home. Marybeth Morley was a complex piece of fluff he didn't have much use for.

He slanted a look in her direction. Granted, she looked a little better than she had that morning. Her hair was combed, her face washed, and her eyes had lost that hung-over look. But he'd been fooled by a drunk before. Never again, he told himself, and turned his attention back to his work.

Within five minutes he knew he'd have the lock installed and the little girl safely secured for the night. But who would take care of the kid after that? Before he left he had to make sure she'd be all right. "Where's Miranda?" he asked.

Marybeth shook the box, emptying the remaining hardware onto her open palm. "In the backyard playing with Timmy." She passed him a screw.

Gunner accepted it but this time was careful not to look at her. "Are you her natural mother?"

"Of course I am," she said indignantly. "Why do you ask?"

He shrugged. "She calls you Marybeth. Most kids call their mothers Mom."

Marybeth sighed as she leaned over to drop the hardware by his knee. "It's a stage she's going through. She thinks it's more mature to call me Marybeth than Mom."

Gunner absorbed that while he pressed his thumb against the latch bolt, testing its resiliency. Satisfied, he picked up the striker frame and held it against the new facing. "Kids can test a person's nerves, that's for sure. Who takes care of her when you're at work?"

Marybeth knew he was fishing, but for what she wasn't sure. She settled her back against the wall to watch him. "Juanita. She's been with us since Miranda's birth." She chuckled, thinking of her housekeeper. "Thank heavens she left for her sister's early this morning and missed all the excitement. She'd have had a tizzy for sure."

"She lives with you?"

"Yes."

She saw the relief on his face and wondered at it.

He gave the brass handle a twist. Now that he knew Miranda was safe, there wasn't a reason to stay. "Works like a charm."

Marybeth stood and dusted off the seat of her shorts. "I really appreciate you doing this for us. How much do I owe you?"

"Nothing," he mumbled, embarrassed that he hadn't fixed the door in the first place as he'd known he should. "It was no trouble."

She pushed her damp bangs from her brow. She was quick to anger, but quicker to forgive. "Well, the least I can do is offer you a beer."

His shoulders tensed. "A little early in the day for a beer, isn't—"

"If you don't hurry, I'm going to have this baby right here in the yard!"

Gunner wheeled just as Miranda rounded the side of the house. She had a suitcase in one hand and was dragging a towheaded little boy by the other. Her stomach looked large enough to give birth to twins at any second.

"Hurry up, Timmy," she cried. "The pains are already three minutes apart. Oh, hi, Gunner." Miranda grinned and dropped Timmy's hand long enough to wave. "Timmy and I are on the way to the hospital. I'm having a baby." She grabbed the boy's hand again. "Come on, Timmy. We'll pretend the sofa is the car."

Gunner gathered his wits enough to step out of the way as the two climbed the porch steps and passed by him on their way into the house.

"If it's a girl, name her after me," Marybeth called after them, laughing, then she turned to Gunner. "I hope your paramedic training included childbirth."

Gunner tore his gaze away from Miranda and the reluctant Timmy to find Marybeth standing beside him, her arms folded across her chest, a smile teasing at her lips. He pulled off his cap and dragged the back of his hand across his brow. The fact that his hand shook a bit didn't surprise him. "Maybe I'll take you up on that beer."

Instead of beer, Gunner opted for the lemonade and cookies Marybeth offered Timmy and Miranda. The four of them sat around the kitchen table while Miranda chattered away. Timmy sat silent and watchful, totally subdued by Miranda's overpowering personality.

It seemed the birth had been successful, Gunner noted, and without his help. Miranda's stomach was flat again. Two pillows lay discarded on the floor beside her chair, proof enough that they—and not a baby—had once filled her shirt. She cradled a doll in her lap.

One by one, Gunner's muscles began to relax. He knew it was stupid, but when he'd heard Miranda's voice and seen her shirt stretched tight over her bulging stomach, for a moment he'd lost all logical thought.

He took a deep, calming breath and immediately his mouth watered as a spicy scent did a fast two-step with his taste buds. The cookies Marybeth had served were good, but he hadn't had a real meal since the night before and that had been interrupted by a grass fire that he'd fought until the wee hours of the morning.

He glanced at the stove where steam bubbled from a pot. "What's cooking?"

"Gumbo," Miranda replied before her mother could speak. "Marybeth makes the best. Want to eat dinner with us tonight?"

Marybeth stood behind Gunner, the lemonade pitcher in hand, ready to refill his glass. She gave Miranda one of those just-wait-until-I-get-you-alone-young-lady looks that Miranda was wise enough to dodge.

"Well, it's the least we can do since he fixed our door," she said in her defense. "Isn't that right, Gunner?"

The kid was a pistol. Gunner couldn't remember the last time he'd smiled this much. And that gumbo sure sounded better than the bologna sandwich that awaited him at home. But what really sold him on the idea was the look he'd seen Marybeth send her daughter. "Sounds fair to me," he replied, and leaned to ruffle the kid's hair. "But first I need to run home and feed my horses."

"Horses!" Miranda was on her feet and hanging on to his elbow. "Do you have horses? Could Timmy and I come with you? We won't get in the way, will we, Timmy? Please, Gunner? Can we please?''

Marybeth glanced nervously out the window then at the kitchen clock. How long did it take to feed horses? They'd been gone nearly two hours already. She paced to the stove and lifted the lid on the pot of gumbo. Steam misted her face.

Miranda was safe, she reassured herself as she stirred bits of okra and shrimp to the surface. No need for her to worry. Gunner was a trusted employee of the local fire department and he had promised to keep a close eye on Miranda. She knew she didn't have to worry about Timmy. He was so shy he wouldn't move unless Gunner told him it was all right. But Miranda?

A shiver worked its way down Marybeth's spine.

A door slammed outside and she dropped the lid back onto the pot and raced for the front of the house. When she reached the door, Gunner was walking up the front walk with Miranda braced on his shoulders. The ball cap Gunner had worn earlier was now on Miranda's head—and backward at that. Both were laughing. Or rather, Gunner was laughing, Miranda was absolutely radiant, giggling and clutching at Gunner's hair.

The sight made Marybeth's breath catch in her throat. For two years she'd worried about her daughter. Ever since Miranda's father's death, the child had charged from one terrifying stage of rebellion to another. But one fact had always remained true: she refused to act like a child. An adult was what she wanted to be, and Marybeth tried her best to deal with this little idiosyncrasy.

When Miranda spotted her mother, she threw both arms above her head and squealed. "Oh, Marybeth, Gunner has the neatest pony named Midnight and he said I could come out and ride him sometime if it's okay with you. Can I, please?"

Marybeth placed a hand on her stomach to still the butterflies that had flapped since the moment the three had left. "We'll see," she said vaguely, stretching her arms up to help Miranda down when Gunner reached her side. Her gaze met his smiling one as she lowered Miranda to the porch. Softened by his interaction with her daughter, she smiled in return. "Dinner's ready, Miranda, so why don't you show Gunner where to wash up."

Tiny bubbles anchored against the sides of the fluted glass. A lazy finger circled the glass's rim, catching a bead of moisture and smearing it round and round, mesmerizing Gunner with its movement. The glass was almost empty. He knew because he'd kept a watchful eye throughout the meal, silently measuring and counting.

He tensed when the hand left the rim and moved to the carafe.

Glass number three. He couldn't just sit there and let the woman drink herself into oblivion. He had to stop her. But how? "Isn't it dangerous to mix wine and fish?" he blurted out.

Marybeth's hand paused in refilling her glass. "That's an old wives' tale," she replied, and topped off her wine. "And it's milk, not wine." She set the carafe on the table and lifted her glass in a silent toast. "Cabernet compliments any seafood."

"Marybeth knows all about foods and wines, 'cause she's an expert," Miranda said proudly. "She writes cookbooks and magazine articles and travels all around the country giving lectures on gourmet cooking."

"Not an expert, Miranda," Marybeth said, embarrassed by her daughter's praise.

"Well, that's what Mamere says," Miranda said defensively.

"Mamere's my mother, and a little prejudiced where Miranda and I are concerned," Marybeth explained for Gunner's benefit. She lifted her wineglass again, but before the glass touched her lips Gunner whisked it from her hand.

"Well, I'm no expert, but that gumbo was the best I've ever had." He dumped the wine down the sink and started gathering plates. "Since you were kind enough to feed me, I'll do the washing up."

Still reeling from having her wineglass all but ripped from her hand, Marybeth stood, as well. "No, please. You're our guest. Miranda, why don't you take Gunner into the living room and entertain him while I clear the table?"

"Okay."

Gunner eyed the carafe while Miranda latched onto his hand, wondering if he had the time—or the nerve—to empty its contents down the sink, as well. There was no telling how many glasses she'd down while she did the dishes. And the housekeeper was still away. If Marybeth got drunk again tonight, who would take care of Miranda?

But Gunner hesitated a second too long. It seemed Miranda took her responsibilities at entertaining seriously, he soon learned. Before he had a chance to grab the carafe, she'd dragged him to the living room, plumped the sofa cushions behind his back, then settled herself in his lap.

"I'll read to you," she told him, and scooped a well-worn book from the end table. "This is the story of Beauty and the Beast. Have you heard it?"

He strained his neck to try to catch a glimpse of Marybeth in the kitchen, but it was no use. The swinging door had already swung shut. "Yeah, but it's been a while," he said, sitting back, reconciled to the fact that he had no choice in the matter but praying like hell Marybeth would leave the wine alone.

"I saw the movie," she said on a sigh. "It was *so* romantic." She flipped to the first page. "I'll be Beauty and you be the Beast."

"I don't know, Miranda," he said hesitantly. "I'm not very good at this kind of thing."

She patted his hand in an offhand manner. "Don't worry. You don't have any lines for a while."

Gunner knew how Timmy must feel. Once Miranda set her mind to something, she was like a director and the world her stage.

She settled back against his chest and began to read. "'Once upon a time, in a faraway land, a young prince lived in a shining castle...'"

The kid is too cute, Gunner thought as he stifled a yawn. She reads with more inflection than an actress trying out for a part.

He inched down on the sofa, seeking a more comfortable position as her voice droned on. "'The Enchantress left behind the rose she had offered him, which would bloom until his twenty-first year. For the spell to be broken, he must learn to love another and earn that person's love in return before the last petal fell. If not, he would remain a beast forever.'" Miranda sighed dreamily as she turned the page.

Gunner tried hard to keep his eyes open, but the combination of a full stomach, too little sleep, and Miranda's voice, lulled him. He'd rest his eyes, he decided, until it was his turn to read.

Twenty minutes later, when Marybeth walked in, Gunner was dead asleep. One arm draped the back of the sofa, the other rested gently on Miranda's hip. His head had fallen back on the sofa and his mouth was slightly agape. Miranda sat on his lap, staring up at him, infatuated.

"Looks like you lost your audience, Miranda," Marybeth whispered, smiling.

"Isn't he just the most handsome man you ever saw?" Miranda whispered back.

In the midst of taking the book from her daughter, Marybeth glanced up. Gunner's face was inches from hers. His eyes were closed, his jaw relaxed, and the most endearing lock of hair curled across his brow. She stepped back and studied him.

Sleep had robbed him of that aloof look he wore so well. His lips were full and moist, and whiskers shadowed a tanned jaw. Asleep he was almost appealing.

His even breathing caught on a soft snore and Marybeth bit back a smile.

"Yes, I do believe he is," she said softly. "Now come on, little lady," she said, pulling the book from Miranda's hand. "It's time for you to scoot off to bed."

"But what about Gunner?" Miranda whispered in concern.

Marybeth straightened and frowned, looking at him again. He was obviously beat, considering he hadn't fluttered so much as an eyelash since she'd entered the room. It would be dangerous to wake him and send him home. He'd probably fall asleep at the wheel and kill himself and she'd have that on her conscious. "I'll let him rest while I get you ready for bed."

When Marybeth returned, Gunner had slipped from his upright position. He now lay sprawled on the sofa with one hand thrown across his eyes. She didn't know much about a fireman's work schedule, but she remembered him telling Miranda during dinner about fighting a grass fire most of the night.

Taking pity on him, she picked up a magazine and curled up on the opposite end of the sofa, dragging an afghan across her legs. She'd let him nap awhile, then send him home.

"Miranda, please," Marybeth whimpered sleepily. "Just a few more minutes, darling, I'm so tired."

Miranda giggled. "Just wait until Mamere hears about this!"

Instantly, Marybeth was awake and kicking at the afghan that covered her. "Hears about what?"

"What the—"

Marybeth jerked upright at the sound of the male voice. Early morning sunlight nearly blinded her as her eyes met Gunner's across the length of the sofa.

Dear, God, Marybeth thought in horror. We've spent the night on the sofa.

"Miranda, this is not what it seems—"

"I'm sorry. I must have fallen asleep and—"

Their words were as tangled as their legs. With every move, Gunner thwarted Marybeth's attempts to rise. Frustrated, she whacked him on the leg. "Will you please!"

The doorbell rang and Miranda skipped off singing, "Don't bother to get up. I'll answer it."

Marybeth heard the door open and Miranda's
squeal of excitement. "Mamere!"

"Oh no," she moaned, and buried her face in her
hands.

Three

— — —

The woman standing in the living room's arched doorway could easily have been the mother of the child standing beside her rather than the grandmother. Mamere. That's what Gunner remembered Miranda calling her. The name sounded French and fit the woman to a tee. She was petite and utterly feminine.

Her gaze moved from Marybeth to Gunner to the rumpled sofa then back to Gunner. The muscles in his neck rolled and twisted to form one tight knot.

"Well, hello."

Although her lips curved in the beginnings of a smile, Gunner heard the hint of surprise in her voice. He didn't dare drop his guard for a minute. He'd never seen a vengeful mother in action—he'd never been caught in such a compromising position himself—but he'd heard enough stories from other guys to know that all hell could break loose at any minute. The purse that swung from her elbow was large enough and looked heavy enough to do as much damage as a frying pan when laid upside the head. He braced himself when she took another step into the room.

"You must be Gunner." She extended her hand, the smile still in place.

"Yes, ma'am," he said, cautiously taking her hand in his. When he would have released it, she held on. He worried for a minute if she might know karate. It wouldn't surprise him, considering his experience with the Morley family thus far.

"Miranda told me all about you last night on the phone." She looked down at her granddaughter who stood at her side, her pride in the child obvious. Then she lifted her gaze again to Gunner. Thankfully, the smile was still in place. "I'm Helene, Miranda's grandmother and Marybeth's mother."

"It's nice to meet you." Gunner gave his hand another gentle tug, but Helene tightened her grip.

"I want to thank you for coming to my girls' rescue." Her smile slowly melted and he could have sworn he saw the glimmer of a tear. "Since they moved to Terrell, I worry so." She placed her free hand on top of their joined ones and squeezed. "But I'm sure you don't want to hear my worries."

Gunner didn't have to ask where Miranda got her gift for gab or her dramatic flair. The proof stood right in front of him. Mamere.

"Mother, really."

Ignoring her daughter, Helene sighed and released his hand. "Frankly, I would have preferred they remain in Dallas." She dropped her purse on a chair and picked up the afghan from the sofa and started to fold it. "But, as I'm sure you're aware, once Marybeth sets her mind to something, there's no stopping her." She gave her daughter a look that would drag a grown man to his knees, but Marybeth simply lifted her chin a notch higher.

Suddenly the woman dropped the afghan and whirled. "My goodness! I'll bet y'all haven't had breakfast yet, have you?" She was already in motion. "I had mine hours ago, but it won't take me a minute to whip together something."

"No, Mother, that isn't necessary. I—"

"Tut-tut. It's no problem at all."

Miranda and Marybeth stole a glance at one another and rolled their eyes. Gunner saw the exchange and wondered at it.

"Besides," Mamere added, turning to frown at Marybeth in disapproval. "You need to freshen up. Why don't you put on that pretty yellow sundress Miranda and I picked out for you," she suggested with a dismissing flick of her hand. She caught Gunner by the elbow, charming him with a smile. "And this handsome man can keep me company in the kitchen while I cook."

"Whoo-ee! You look like something the cat dragged in."

Gunner frowned at Joe as he slid into the booth opposite him. He'd considered skipping his usual stop at Rosie's Café for morning coffee, but he knew if he did, Joe would only show up at the farm later to check up on him. He lifted a hand and motioned for Rosie to bring him a cup. Might as well get the inquisition over with now. "Good morning to you, too."

"Trying to grow a beard?"

Self-consciously, Gunner smoothed a hand across his jaw. "Nah. Haven't had time to shave, is all."

Joe nodded, looking for all the world like the cat who'd swallowed the canary. "Yeah, I guess you've been pretty busy." He lifted his hands out of the way as Rosie leaned across the table to slide a cup of coffee in front of Gunner.

"Thanks, Rosie."

"Anything else, Chief?"

"Yeah, bring me the special, sunny-side up." He picked up the jar of sugar and sprinkled a liberal amount into his cup.

"That woman swings a mean right, doesn't she?"

Gunner glanced up. "Rosie?"

"No, the Morley woman."

Gunner touched a tentative finger to his eye. Since he hadn't looked in a mirror in nearly two days, he hadn't a clue how the eye looked, but it was still as tender as hell. "Yeah, she does," Gunner muttered, and picked up the spoon to stir.

"Get her door fixed?"

The spoon flipped out of his hand, slopping coffee over the cup's side. He took his time mopping it up. "What makes you think I went back over there and fixed her door?"

Joe shrugged, biting back a smile. "Well, I sort of drove by the place yesterday afternoon—just to make sure she'd found someone to do the work, you understand. Saw your truck parked out front." He reared back against the orange Naugahyde booth and chuckled. "Being as how the two of you were all cozied up on the front porch, holding hands and all, I just cruised on by."

Heat flooded Gunner's face. "We weren't holding hands. She hurt her finger working on the door and I was just checking it out."

"Break anything?"

"Just a fingernail."

"Oh," Joe said knowingly, "that explains it."

Gunner set his cup down with a thump. "If you've got something to say, say it, and quit pussyfooting around."

Joe's hands came up, palms up, in surrender. "I'm not trying to say anything. It just struck me as odd that your truck was over there yesterday afternoon and still there this morning."

"Hell, Joe, you're wasting your time with the fire department. You ought to be a damn private eye." Rosie arrived with his plate and Gunner held his tongue while she placed it in front of him. Rosie's Café was the center of the town gossip mill and Rosie the head miller. Wouldn't do to feed her a new chaff of scandal to grind. Dealing with Joe's tongue was difficult enough.

"And to put your dirty little mind to rest," he said as soon as Rosie was out of earshot. "My truck was still there because I fell asleep on the sofa."

"Alone?"

A new shiny spot was worn on the orange Naugahyde while Gunner squirmed under Joe's expectant gaze. "No," he finally admitted. "She fell asleep, too. But this isn't what you think," he was quick to add.

"Why don't you just tell me the whole story from beginning to end?"

Gunner did. From repairing the door, to eating dinner, through story time with Miranda and ending with Mamere's unexpected appearance that morning.

"I'm plumb worn out from two-stepping that woman's prying questions. And starved to death, besides. You'd think she could cook, being as how her daughter writes cookbooks and teaches cooking. But she kept shoving food in front of me that was either bland, burnt, or unrecognizable." At the memory, Gunner pushed back his plate, his appetite gone.

Joe let out a long, low whistle. "Man, you got trouble."

Gunner cocked his head toward Joe, his eyes narrowed suspiciously. "Trouble? What do you mean, trouble?"

"Does a daddy and a shotgun spark any fear?"

Gunner waved away his friend's concern with a tired hand. "It's not like that at all. Marybeth's mother didn't even bat an eye at seeing me there and it was obvious we'd spent the night together on the sofa. Makes me wonder if her daughter doesn't make a habit of entertaining men all night." Gunner shook his head, his mind trailing off to Miranda. "Poor kid. What kind of example is that for a girl her age?"

Marybeth stopped midstride, one foot in the house, one on the porch, her hand still gripping the new brass doorknob. Something was different. She felt it, but she couldn't quite put her finger on exactly what that something was.

She took a step back and scanned the front of the house. When she'd left for Atlanta three days before, the door facing had been repaired, but unpainted. Now the new wood gleamed a Williamsburg blue, the same shade as her shutters.

Baffled by the change, she touched a finger to the door facing, testing to see if the paint was wet, but her finger came away dry. *Did Mr. Peters sober up and remember he hadn't finished the job?* she wondered. Groaning, she stepped across the threshold. No, knowing her mother, she'd probably taken charge as soon as Marybeth was out of sight and hired someone to come and finish the job.

"Miranda! I'm home," she called, dropping her garment bag on the entry hall floor. "Miranda!" she called again as she headed for the back of the house.

In the kitchen, Juanita lifted her head, her hands buried in dough, a welcoming smile blooming on her face. "*Buenos dias,* Señora Morley. You are home early."

Marybeth slung an arm around the housekeeper's shoulder and hugged her to her. "Hi, Juanita. I caught an early flight. What's cooking?"

"Cinnamon rolls. How was the trip?"

"Fine." She dipped a finger into the bowl of glaze waiting to top the finished rolls only to have Juanita slap it away. "Who did Mother hire to paint the door facing?" she asked before popping the finger into her mouth and sucking at the smidgen of sugary glaze she'd managed to snag.

"Oh, your mother, she didn't hire anyone. Señor Gunner did the painting."

"Gunner!"

"*Si.* Such a nice man," she said, smiling as she rolled the dough out flat. "He came by Monday after you left and took a paint sample from the shutters. Then, yesterday, he returned and painted. Miranda helped," she added, her smile broadening. "The little one had more paint on her nose than on the door. I worried she might be in his way, but he said to leave her with him. She was his helper. A nice man," she repeated with a decisive nod of her head.

Nice man, my rear end, Marybeth thought irritably. Personally, she was a little sick of hearing his name. Ever since he'd left her house Sunday morning, she'd heard nothing but Gunner this and Gunner that. Miranda was absolutely besotted with the man and her mother sang his praises as if he was the best thing since sliced bread.

Well, he may have had snowed her daughter, her mother, and now her housekeeper with his charming ways, but he hadn't fooled her. In her mind, he was still overbearing, rude, and a little too pushy. The painting of her door only confirmed that opinion.

"Where is Miranda?"

"In her room. She has a date," Juanita said, chuckling as she twisted the lengths of dough into shape.

"A date?"

"Yes, Señor Gunner is taking her to dinner."

"He's what!"

The anger in Marybeth's voice had Juanita dropping the dough and wringing her flour-covered hands. "Please don't be angry, Señora Morley. I called your mother to ask if Miranda could go and she said it would be okay."

Mamere strikes again. "Don't worry, Juanita," Marybeth said through tight lips. "I'll handle this." She headed for Miranda's room.

But Miranda's room was empty. Without missing a step Marybeth marched straight to her own room and the dressing area beyond, knowing full well that was where she'd find her daughter.

Miranda stood in front of the mirrored closet door, twisting this way and that, admiring the way her mother's red sequined cocktail dress billowed around her legs. Her hair was piled on top of her head, anchored there by a rhinestone clip. More rhinestones glittered at her ears and at her throat.

"Miranda! What do you think you're doing?" Marybeth demanded to know.

The child wheeled, nearly falling out of her mother's heels. "Hi, Marybeth! Guess what? I have a date with Gunner."

"So I heard." Marybeth crossed to the vanity and pulled out the chair. She dropped down and pulled Miranda to stand in front of her. She knew she'd have to be careful, that she was dealing with a tender ego and an extremely delicate situation. But she also knew she had to put an end to this infatuation with Gunner Keith.

"Listen, Miranda," she said patiently. "I know you like Gunner, and he likes you, but I don't think it's a good idea for you to go out to dinner with him."

"But why?" she cried out, tears filling her eyes.

"Well," Marybeth said slowly, racking her brain to think of a plausible excuse, something Miranda would accept. "Gunner's a grown man, sweetheart, and you're still a little girl, too young to date just yet."

"But, Marybeth, you don't understand, he's not—"

The doorbell rang, interrupting her. "Oh no," Miranda cried, clapping her hands at her cheeks. "He's here." Her gaze flew to the mirror and she dropped her chin, sniffing back tears. "I can't let him see me looking like this. My mascara is all messed up."

Marybeth tipped up her daughter's chin. The disappointment in the face that met hers nearly broke her heart. "You look gorgeous, sweetheart, but if it'll make you feel better, why don't you wash your face and I'll go talk to Gunner."

By the time Marybeth reached the front of the house, Juanita had already answered the door and ushered Gunner into the living room.

She was standing opposite him, her hands clasped at her breasts. "Señor Gunner, you look so handsome!" she was saying. "My little Miranda's heart will be stolen for sure." The distant buzzing sound of the oven's timer had her hands fluttering above her head. "*Mi Dias!* The cinnamon rolls. I baked especially for you. You must not leave without them," she said, wagging a teasing finger in his face. She turned to leave, but when she saw Marybeth standing in the doorway, the smile disappeared. Pursing her lips, she lifted her chin and sailed past Marybeth, muttering something in Spanish under her breath.

Gunner had caught sight of Marybeth at the same moment as Juanita. He told himself the sudden catch in his breath was the unexpectedness of seeing her for he'd been told she wouldn't be home until late . . . but the truth was Marybeth herself had stolen his breath. T-shirts and baggy shorts, that was all he'd ever seen her wear. Even after her mother had instructed her to put on the sundress Sunday morning, she'd come back wearing jeans and a man's shirt, an act of defiance he could almost understand since he'd met Mamere.

Now she wore a dress. A gauzy thing, full-skirted, and hanging nearly to her ankles, with every color of the rainbow bleeding from one vibrant hue to the next.

A brass belt hugged her waist, gold sandals strapped her toes.

And her eyes fairly snapped in anger.

"Hello, Marybeth," he said, finding his voice and wondering what the hell had her so riled up.

"Gunner," she acknowledged, and gestured for him to sit on the sofa. Taking the chair opposite him, she filled her lungs with a deep breath. He'd already ascertained she didn't have much upstairs, but the V-necked dress showed a surprising amount of cleavage. He avoided the inviting view, and focused on her face. "We have a problem," she was saying.

"Problem?" he repeated in confusion as he watched her fingers move to nervously pleat the folds of her skirt across her lap.

"Yes." She took a another deep breath and plunged on. "I'm sure your intentions with Miranda are purely innocent, but she is young and impressionable and has this huge crush on you. She thinks this dinner thing is a date, like boyfriend and girlfriend, and she has been primping all afternoon to impress you." Her eyes filled and Gunner knew real fear. He'd never been any good at handling hysterical females. But what she was saying was wrong. Dead wrong.

"Marybeth, I don't mean to contradict you, but I think you're jumping to the wrong conclusion here."

"I am not!" she exclaimed indignantly. "Miranda is in my room right this minute dressed in my clothes and putting on makeup."

Gunner tried to hide a smile as an image of Miranda all dolled up formed in his mind. "She's just dressing her part."

It was Marybeth's turn to look confused. "What part?"

"Beauty. And I'm the Beast. You know, the book she was reading the other night. She's just playing pretend."

Marybeth wanted to believe him, but she knew Miranda. She'd seen the look on her daughter's face when she'd told her she couldn't go. The child was way beyond her years and wanted nothing more than to be a grown-up. Her infatuation with Gunner had to be stopped. Stiffening her spine, Marybeth said, "I disagree."

"Well, that's your privilege. So what do you expect me to do about this?"

"Go home. Stay away from Miranda. She'll get over this in time."

"But I promised her dinner. I don't want to disappoint her."

"I realize that, but surely you can see the wisdom in—"

"Hello, Gunner." Miranda stepped into the room, her eyes downcast. She approached the sofa, her lower lip quivering. "I'm sorry I can't go to dinner with you tonight. Marybeth says you're too old for me." She stopped when she reached his knee.

He swallowed back the biggest wad of emotion he'd experienced in a long time. He had to think of some way to pull this off or the kid was going to break his heart.

He caught Miranda's hand in his and when her tiny little fingers folded around his, he felt another fissure open in his chest. "Now I don't want to go against your mother's wishes," he said, slowly devising a plan as he went. "And whatever she says goes, but maybe she'd reconsider if we had a chaperone." He shifted his gaze to Marybeth's, daring her to disagree, but inwardly begging her to understand. "What about it, Marybeth? What if you went along? Maybe you could be the wicked old witch or something."

That was exactly who she felt like, too, Marybeth reflected petulantly. The wicked old witch. She sipped at her wine, enjoying a pity party for one, as she watched Gunner swirl Miranda around the dance floor. From the moment they'd entered the restaurant, the two of them had charmed everyone in the place.

She'd have thought a man like him would be embarrassed to be seen with Miranda, dressed as she was. Instead he'd escorted her to their table as if she were visiting royalty, stopping to speak to acquaintances along the way and introducing her as his friend, Princess Miranda from the Kingdom of Morley.

And Miranda had loved every minute of it.

Even now, as he spun her around and around the small dance floor, her face was flushed with excitement. The skirt of the red sequined dress swirled around her little legs with each fast twirl, and the light glanced off her rhinestones making them glitter like real diamonds, just the way she had dreamed. Marybeth knew about the dream, for she'd heard it recounted countless times and had even watched Miranda reenact the fantasy, smiling up at her imaginary prince as she danced around the living room alone.

Marybeth clung hard to her anger. She wanted to be mad at Gunner. To find some excuse, some fault with the man to justify the anger. But she couldn't, which made her feel even more like the wicked witch he'd suggested.

She took another sip of her wine and sighed, letting her anger go as she watched them dance. She had to give him credit for he'd certainly done his part in making the evening a magical one for Miranda. A suit, a tie, the best restaurant in town.

And the manners of a nobleman.

He does look like a prince, she admitted grudgingly as she noted the way he filled out the black Western-cut suit. Everything about the way he carried himself, even while dancing, screamed masculinity and authority... and whispered something else, she realized, sitting up straighter in her chair. A wildness, an untamed sexuality.

A shiver worked its way down her spine as she studied him in profile, searching for clues that hinted at this wildness. He was looking down at Miranda, the expression on his face smiling and indulgent. She couldn't see his eyes, but knew they'd be that soft brown, the same color they'd been when he'd examined her hand the day they'd repaired her door.

But she knew how his eyes could change with his mood. From warm chocolate to a dark turbulent brown. The first morning they'd met, when he'd held her pinned against the wall, his eyes had been dark, smoldering with rage. She'd seen the change at other times, as well, and experienced an answering response in her own pulse rate.

Juanita had called him handsome, and to be honest she had to admit he was. Coal-black hair, features so well defined they appeared to be carved by an artist's knife. Arms strong enough to squeeze the breath out of a person if he so desired.

Yet there was something about him that made a woman want to be in those arms. To rake her fingers through his hair, to nip at those brooding lips and taste the savage promise she somehow knew was there.

She swallowed hard as the song ended and the two approached the table. She wanted to blame the wine for the sudden dryness in her mouth, the thundering of her pulse ... and knew she couldn't.

When they reached the table, Gunner stretched out a hand to pull out Miranda's chair and his arm brushed Marybeth's. Fire leaped beneath her skin and flooded her face with color at the brief contact.

"Oh, Marybeth, isn't this the most wonderful night ever?" Miranda gushed.

Wonderful? Maybe for Miranda. For her it was a nightmare, an awakening of emotions she'd thought she'd buried with her husband years before. She should have listened to her mother, she reflected ruefully, and taken a lover months ago. Perhaps then she wouldn't be salivating over Gunner like some love-starved fool.

"Yes, it is, darling," she said, ignoring her own feelings and thinking only of her daughter.

"Gunner is absolutely, positively the best dancer in the world! You *have* to dance with him."

"Oh, I don't think so, sweetheart," she replied hastily. "I'm sure he needs a rest."

"Oh, he doesn't mind, do you, Gunner?" Miranda insisted, turning to him. "Marybeth loves to dance. She and my daddy used to go dancing all the time."

Needing an anchor in the storm of emotion raging through her, Marybeth latched onto her wineglass. "That was years ago, Miranda, and if you'll remember, Daddy always complained I tried to lead. Besides, this is your night. I'm just here as the wicked old witch."

Gunner took the wineglass from her hand and set it on the table. It wasn't the first time he'd pulled a glass from Marybeth's hand, but before she could take issue with the matter, he was tugging her to her feet. "Even the wicked old witch is entitled to one dance."

"Oh, no, please," Marybeth begged. "I'll step all over your feet."

"I'll take my chances."

"Go on, Marybeth. Dance with him," Miranda encouraged.

Realizing that arguing wasn't doing her any good and Miranda would be disappointed if she refused, Marybeth followed him to the square of parquet, reminding herself it was only a dance. But when his arm circled her waist, her knees nearly buckled.

He took her hand in his and lifted a brow in question. "Would you like to lead or shall I?"

The question stiffened her knees and brought her anger singing back. Why did the man always have to say or do something to irritate her? Why couldn't he be nice to her, as he was to Miranda?

"I guess we could flip for it," she replied sarcastically.

Gunner tossed back his head and laughed. The sound was low and throaty, totally masculine, and pulsed beneath Marybeth's skin. "I'm fresh out of quarters," he said, one side of his mouth quirked up in a smile. "Why don't I start, but feel free to take over anytime."

She didn't like it when he smiled. It was easier to be angry with him when he frowned at her as was his usual habit.

She didn't like the way he danced, either, she concluded after only two steps. She'd expected him to hold her as he had Miranda—at arm's length. But he insisted on pulling her flush against him, tucking her head beneath his chin. She thought she detected the beat of his heart, but she couldn't be sure, her own was nearly pounding out of her chest. She closed her eyes in an attempt to blank out the sensation of his body moving against hers. This was horrible. This was hell. This was the most glorious feeling she'd experienced in years.

She'd acknowledged his skill at dancing from a distance, but it was nothing like experiencing it firsthand. There was a sureness to his movements, a naturalness that defied the size of the man. Against her will, her body relaxed against him, anticipating and matching his every move.

How long had it been since she'd felt the heat of a man's body against her own? Two years? Nearly three? Too long, she decided as her fingers found their way to the nape of his neck. Hair as black as sin curled seductively around her fingertips. He spun her in a tight circle, making her laugh, and she clung to him, dizzy with the sensations pulsing through her.

Much too soon the song ended and he stopped moving. A good five seconds hummed between them before he released her. As they stepped apart, he kept her hand firmly in his. Confused, she sought his gaze...and found a new emotion in those brown eyes. Passion burned there, dark and haunting, pulling at her like nothing had ever pulled at her in her life.

"Thanks for the dance," he said, his voice husky and low.

She felt herself drawn toward him, not by any move on his part, but by some need buried deep within herself. Something primitive and wild, totally out of her control. She rose to her toes, her eyelids too heavy to hold up any longer, and lifted her face to his. This can't be happening, her logical mind screamed. A man cannot make a woman feel this way with a simple look and a touch.

But Gunner had.

How? And why? She clutched at his arm, nearly stumbling as she caught herself before pressing her lips to his. She rocked back on her feet, searching his face for a clue, and watched his lip curl in disgust.

He's toying with me, she realized, thoroughly humiliated. Like a cat playing with a mouse. Well, two can play as easily as one, she decided. No one made a fool of Marybeth Morley.

Jerking her hand free of his, she caught her skirt between her fingertips and dipped her knees in a low curtsy. "My pleasure, my lord," she said, smiling sweetly.

A smattering of applause came from the tables near the dance floor and, tossing her head back with a laugh, Marybeth turned to curtsy to the people there, as well.

She glanced back over her shoulder at Gunner. "Not bad for a wicked old witch, huh?"

Four

—

"**D**on't you leave lights on when you know you're going to be out after dark?"

The derision in his voice fanned Marybeth's anger a little higher. The sanctimonious bastard. Did he never tire of finding fault with everything she did? Heaving an exasperated breath, she pushed past him, tugging her key ring from her purse.

She rammed the front door key at the lock and missed. Muttering a choice word, she squinted her eyes in the darkness and tried to make out the lock's narrow opening. She thrust the key again. And missed. Dammit! Why hadn't Juanita thought to leave the front porch light on before she'd left?

"Here, let me try."

Furious, Marybeth shoved his hand away. "I don't need your help." She stabbed again at the lock and this time the key slipped in. She couldn't resist tossing a smug look over her shoulder. "See? I told you I didn't need your help."

Gunner stepped back and waited while Marybeth attempted to turn the key in the lock.

"What's the matter now?" he asked from behind her.

"The darn thing won't turn!" Marybeth wiggled the key in the mechanism and twisted again.

"Is that the new key?"

Immediately, Marybeth tensed. Why hadn't she thought of that? Of course the door wouldn't open, because she was using the old key on the new lock. She yanked it out and started flipping through the ring. "No. It's the old one. I have the new one right—" She dropped her hand, her shoulders slumping in defeat.

"What?"

"It's on the kitchen counter. I meant to put it on my key ring, but I forgot."

"Can't you just ring the doorbell and get Juanita to let y'all in?"

"No, I can't just ring the doorbell and get Juanita to let us in," she mimicked sarcastically. "She isn't home. She's gone to her sister's."

"Well how do you propose to get into the house?"

"I don't know," Marybeth said, impatiently pushing at her bangs. "Maybe if you'd be quiet a minute and give me a chance to think, I could come up with something."

Gunner stepped back, aligning himself with Miranda. He crossed his arms across his chest and pressed his lips together.

Racking her brain for a means of entrance, Marybeth crossed to the living-room window and peered through the pane. Even in the darkness, she could see the window latch was in place. And even if it wasn't and she was able to raise it, she knew the elaborate burglar alarm her mother had had installed would go off and the police would be at her house within minutes. She didn't think she was up to another confrontation with the city's emergency services!

"Gunner could break the door down like he did the last time," Miranda suggested helpfully.

Marybeth all but shuddered. "No, thank you." She crossed back to the door and studied it. After a full minute of heavy silence, she turned to Gunner. She'd rather bite off her tongue than ask for his help, but it seemed she had no other alternative.

"Have you got any suggestions?"

"Sure you want my help?"

Marybeth swallowed an angry retort. Wasn't it just like the man to make her crawl? "I wouldn't have asked if I didn't."

Slowly he unfolded his arms and stretched out a hand. "Give me your keys."

Her fingers curled defensively around the key ring. "Why?"

"Unless you changed all the locks on your house to match the new one on the front door, then that key should still open the back door."

"Oh," Marybeth said in a small voice.

"Give me the key and I'll go around back and open up. You and Miranda wait here and I'll let you in the front."

Marybeth clung to the ring as she headed for the porch steps. "That won't be necessary. We'll just go with you. Come on, Miranda."

Gunner caught her by the elbow before she'd taken two steps. "And trip over something in the process and break your neck." He dropped her elbow and held out his hand again. "Just give me the keys."

Glaring at him in the darkness, Marybeth slapped them into his hand then whirled away from him to stand by Miranda.

"Isn't he wonderful?" Miranda whispered almost reverently as she watched him disappear into the darkness.

"Yes, he is, isn't he," Marybeth said aloud, but to herself repeated, *the sanctimonious bastard.*

Moments later she heard the thud of his footsteps across the wooden entry hall floor, then the faint click of metal as he unlocked the door. The porch light flicked on, nearly blinding her.

She grabbed Miranda's hand and stepped across the threshold as soon as the door swung open, tugging her daughter behind her. Forcing a smile, she turned, placing Gunner between herself and the open door, hoping the man could take a hint. "Thank you for getting us into the house and for the lovely evening," she said graciously.

"My pleasure, ma'am." Gunner hunkered down to tweak Miranda under the chin. "How 'bout you, Princess? Did you get enough dancing to suit you?"

Miranda fought back a yawn. "Yes, thanks, Gunner."

He chuckled, seeing that she was almost dead on her feet. "You ought to sleep like a rock tonight."

"Mmm-hmm," she mumbled sleepily. She pulled her hand from her mother's, leaned over and pressed her lips to his cheek. "Good night, Gunner. You make a really neat Beast."

A lump formed in his throat as his hand went to touch the spot on his cheek.

Miranda yawned again and looked up at her mother. "I think I'll go to bed now, Marybeth," she said as she turned away. "Good night."

"Good night, darling."

Gunner pushed his hands against his knees and stood. "Cute kid," he murmured as he watched Miranda disappear down the hall.

"Yes, she is," Marybeth repeated on a sigh, her anger with Gunner for the moment forgotten. She turned to him, finding a smile to offer in way of a truce. "I can't thank you enough for your kindness to Miranda."

In the porch light, he noticed the flush on her cheeks and the overbright gleam in her eyes and remembered Juanita was gone for the night. "A cup of coffee would be thanks enough," he suggested, thinking the added caffeine would probably keep him up half the night but might go a long way in diluting the alcohol in Marybeth's system.

"It's awfully late," she replied hesitantly.

Gunner glanced at his watch. "It's not quite ten."

Softened by his interaction with Miranda, she capitulated. "Oh, why not," she said, and led the way to the kitchen.

She opened a cupboard and pulled out her grinder. "What's your pleasure?" she asked with a wave at a line of labeled jars filled with beans.

"Don't you have just regular old coffee?"

A niggling of the old annoyance returned and she fought it back. "No," she said patiently. "I only keep gourmet blends on hand. So what'll it be?"

"Whatever you have is fine with me."

"Good. I'm having Irish coffee." With that settled, she started gathering ingredients. Her head and one hand in the refrigerator searching for whipped cream, she asked, "Will you grab a bottle of whiskey from under the bar in the living room?"

"Whiskey? What for?"

"For the Irish coffee, you goose," she said on a laugh.

"Can't you make it without it?"

Puzzled by his reluctance, Marybeth pulled her head out of the refrigerator and turned to stare at him. "Do you have a problem with liquor or something?"

"Not with liquor. Only people who abuse it."

Slowly Marybeth straightened as events began to click into place. Gunner's taking her glass from her hand, pouring her wine down the sink. She started toward him. "And you think I abuse it, don't you?" she asked, coming to a stop in front of him.

"Well," he replied, wishing like hell he'd never asked for the coffee in the first place. "The signs are all there."

"What signs?"

"Hangovers to start with and—"

"*What* hangovers?"

"The morning we busted in here, you were nursing a pretty good one."

"I wasn't suffering from a hangover, you big baboon," she said angrily, planting her fists on her hips. "I had jet lag! I'd been in California for a week and didn't get home until three in the morning." She stabbed at his chest with the tip of her index finger, forcing him to fall back a step. "What else?" she demanded.

"You offered me a beer."

"I was being polite." She poked him again and he found himself backed up against the kitchen counter. "What else?" she demanded angrily.

"The wine—"

"I have an occasional glass of wine with a meal. So what?"

"Three glasses."

"You counted?" she asked in disbelief.

"Yeah."

"Why?"

"I didn't want you to get drunk again and leave Miranda unprotected. Hell, Marybeth. She's just a kid. If you get drunk and pass out, who's going to look after her?"

"So you poured my wine down the sink?"

"Yes," he replied.

"And tonight you took my wineglass away for the same reason?"

"I thought you'd had enough. I'm just sorry I didn't grab it sooner."

"But I wasn't drunk," she said, denying his implication.

"You definitely weren't feeling any pain on the dance floor."

She folded her arms at her breasts. "I was having a good time," she said through tight lips.

"And nearly fell on your face."

Remembering how she'd stumbled when she'd stopped just short of making a complete fool of herself, she said, "I wasn't drunk, you imbecile. I was catching myself from kissing you!"

"Kissing me?"

"Yes, and thank God I came to my senses in time."
She whirled from him, but he caught her elbow, pulling her back.

"You were going to kiss me? Why?"

Embarrassed now and unable to look at him, she tried to pull away. "I don't know. I guess I just got caught up in the moment."

His hand slipped from her elbow, to her wrist, catching her hand in his. "Do you always kiss the men you dance with?"

Marybeth's chest swelled in anger as her head snapped up to meet his gaze. "You don't have a very high opinion of me, do you, Gunner?"

"It's climbing by the minute," he said as his thumb slid to the palm of her hand and gently massaged. Her pulse throbbed beneath his fingers while his gaze roamed her face, searching for God only knew what. "You could kiss me now," he suggested softly.

She wet her suddenly dry lips. She didn't like the look in his eyes. They'd turned to that soft brown and reflected the same passion she'd seen at the restaurant after their dance. "I don't want to kiss you."

"I think you do."

Because he was right, she tried to wrench her hand from his. "You overinflated baboon! I wouldn't kiss you if—"

His lips silenced her as he shifted to catch her in the circle of his arms. Her eyes bugged wide to find his were closing, his lashes brushing her cheekbones in a butterfly-light caress. She worked her hands between their bodies, intent on pushing at his chest, but instead her fingers curled into his shirt and clung.

Her surrender was slow, sensual. Gunner tasted the first hint of it on her lips . . . and found the courage to seek more. Her yielding carried further, a slow torturous arch starting with her breasts as she melted against first his chest, then his groin. The sensation sent lightning bolts ripping through him ... and the edge of the kitchen counter cutting into his back. But the pain in his back was nothing compared to the wrenching his libido was getting.

He knew he should stop, or at least come up for air, but damn she tasted good. And felt even better. His hands roamed her back from the nape of her neck to her waist, his fingers snagging on the gauzy fabric of her blouse and making him wish for bare skin. She was a little slip of a thing, not much more than a handful, but he sensed something powerful within her, something stronger than he'd experienced with any other woman.

"Marybeth?" he whispered against her lips.

"Hmm?" was all she managed in response.

"You've cast a spell on me, you witch," he said and nipping at her lower lip.

Her eyelids flipped up. *Witch?* Taking a step back, she looked at him, unconsciously balling her hand into a fist. *A drunk, a hussy, and now a witch.* Marybeth had had about all the abuse she could take from this man.

"Yes, I have," she said, feigning a smile. "And you, my dear, are now a frog." She punched him as hard as she could in the stomach, then stormed from the room, leaving him doubled over and gasping for air.

"The sanctimonious bastard," Marybeth muttered to herself as she paced back and forth in her room. Her knuckles ached and her fingers tingled from the blow she'd delivered to Gunner's solar plexus. But he'd deserved it, she told herself, rubbing at her sore hand. He'd all but called her a drunk and a hussy, then had the nerve to kiss her and blame the resulting passion on her by saying she was a witch and had cast a spell on him. And what had she done to deserve any of his accusations? Nothing. Absolutely nothing.

She'd never had a hangover in her life, although at the moment getting roaring drunk sounded pretty good. As far as his suggestion that she was free with her favors toward men...well, good grief! She hadn't been with a man since Tom had died! She'd been too busy earning a living and taking care of Miranda.

Her steps slowed and at the foot of the bed, she stopped and sank down on the peach comforter. Her lip quivered and tears burned behind her eyes. The truth was, since Tom had died she hadn't *wanted* to be with any other man.

Until Gunner.

She heard the back door slam and the first tear slipped from her lid and coursed miserably down her face. He was gone. She bit down hard on her lower lip to keep the tears at bay. She didn't want to cry. She didn't want to *want*. The *tears* she knew she could control, but the *want* just wouldn't go away.

She fell back on the bed, hugging her arms around her chest, and let the tears come, hoping that in the flood the want would wash away.

Gunner drove. Not because he needed the practice or had any particular destination in mind. He just drove, needing to clear his head and calm his temper. Was the woman crazy or what?

She'd wanted to kiss him. She'd admitted as much. And she sure as hell hadn't complained during the actual act. It was afterwards when her mood had done a smooth one-hundred-and-eighty, that she'd belted him hard in the gut.

"Women," he muttered irritably as he approached Rosie's Café. "Who needs 'em?" He slowed the truck, his gaze cutting across the parking lot. Trucks outnumbered the cars parked there nearly two-to-one. And most of those trucks were red. Fire-engine red. Looked like half the volunteer fire department had chosen to stop in at Rosie's before calling it a night. Something must be up, he decided, and whipped into an empty space in the back row.

As he crossed the parking lot, he couldn't help chuckling. Not only were the trucks painted red, they boasted every option known to man. Over-wide tires, a minimum of three antennae, a light bar with two cherries on top. These men took their jobs seriously and what the city couldn't provide, they supplied out of their own funds. Gunner hated to think what he'd do without any one of them.

Shaking his head, he pushed open the glass door, sending the cowbell attached to it clanging. Every head in the place turned as if on cue. A wolf whistle ripped through the air. "Hey, Chief! Hot date or are you preaching somewhere tonight?" A roar of laughter rose from the crowded tables and Gunner's cheeks flamed a hot pink. He glanced down at his suit and wished like hell he'd kept driving.

Scowling, he slipped into the booth opposite Joe. "Don't you guys have anything better to do than sit around soaking up Rosie's coffee?"

"We're having a board meeting, Chief."

"B-o-a-r-d or b-o-r-e-d?"

"Board, as in the business kind," J.D., the unoffi-cial spokesman of the group replied. "You men-tioned the other day we needed a Jaws of Life and we were thinking maybe we could raise the funds by sponsoring a chili cook-off. Joe here—" he said, waving a hand Joe's way "—suggested we offer a challenge between the volunteers and some of the town's service organizations."

Gunner nodded, naturally liking any idea that pro-duced new equipment for the fire department, but liking it better because it took the spotlight off him. "Sounds good to me. The Jaycees are usually primed for a challenge."

"Those turkeys wouldn't know chili from dog food." J.D. laughed and slapped Gunner on the back as he stood. "Come on, boys. The Jaycees are meet-ing over at Carmona's tonight. Perfect time to hit on 'em. You coming, Joe?"

"Nah, I'll stay and keep Gunner company."

While the men trooped out, laughing and jostling one another, Gunner tugged at his tie, loosening it enough to undo his shirt's top button. He took the first good breath he'd had all evening and caught Joe staring at him.

"Do I have pie on my face or something?" Gunner asked.

Joe chuckled. "No, just lipstick."

Gunner's hand flew to his mouth, the back of it wiping across his lips.

"No, more to the left," Joe said. Using his own cheek as a guide, he scrunched his mouth to one side and pointed to a spot on the lower side of his cheek.

Flustered, Gunner jerked a napkin from the container on the table and scrubbed. "Did I get it?"

Joe nodded and grinned. "Yeah. I wouldn't have said anything, but the color just didn't go with your tie."

Gunner growled an unintelligible response.

"Things must be picking up between you and the Morley woman. First hand-holding and now kissing. Your sex life is definitely improving."

"My sex life is none of your damn business."

"Didn't say it was," Joe replied in a lazy drawl. "Just commenting."

"I'd appreciate it if in the future you'd keep your comments to yourself," Gunner replied tersely.

"Sure thing, Chief. Whatever you say." Joe picked up his cup and sipped. "The boys are really pumped up about this chili cook-off."

"Good. We can use the equipment."

"That's a fact." Joe toyed with his cup, his forehead plowing in deep thought. "A lot of work goes into planning one of these shindigs. Time, place, entry fees, judges." He took a sip, his frown deepening before he glanced up at Gunner. "Didn't you say the Morley woman was a famous chef or something? Since y'all are such good friends and all, maybe you could ask her to judge and—"

Gunner pressed one palm to his stomach, his last tangle with Marybeth still fresh on his mind. He shoved the other about three inches from Joe's nose. "Don't even think it."

"Why not?"

"I wouldn't ask that she-cat the time of day."

"Why?"

" 'Cause she belted me one."

Joe's eyes widened in surprise. "Did you molest her or something?"

Gunner squirmed in his seat while he stole a glance around the room, wishing Joe would keep his voice down. "No, I just kissed her."

Joe lifted his face and hooted at the ceiling. "And she belted you one?"

"Right square in the stomach." Gunner shook his head. "Women. Who can figure 'em?" He planted his forearms on the table and leaned across it, his tone conspiratorial. "Just between you and me, Joe, I think the woman's a nut case. One minute she's cuddled up against me all soft and warm and the next she's spitting fire and swinging her fist."

Joe settled back in the booth, biting back a smile. "Women are a puzzle, that's for sure. But I wouldn't take it personally, Chief. Maybe it's the alcohol. Didn't you say she was a drunk?"

"I thought she was." Gunner dragged a hand through his hair. "Hell, I don't know. She says she didn't have a hangover that morning we busted in her door, she said she was suffering from jet lag."

"Could've been," Joe replied, reaching for his cup.

A frown bunched up the skin above Gunner's nose. "Yeah, maybe." He slapped his hands against the table. "Hell, I don't know. But she's driving me crazy. One minute she's sweet as sugar and the next she's flying off in a rage. She's a witch," he said, leaning back and tugging at his tie. "And I told her as much."

His cup of coffee halfway to his mouth, Joe slowly lowered it back to the table without tasting it. "You called her a witch?"

"Yeah."

"Before or after she belted you?"

"Before." Puzzled, Gunner leaned closer. "Why?"

Joe shook his head as he blew out a long breath. "Chief, we need to talk about your technique."

"I'm *not* calling her."

Joe reached for the phone. "Then I will."

Gunner clamped his hand over Joe's, preventing him from lifting the receiver. "And you're not calling her, either."

Joe dragged his hand from beneath Gunner's and reared his chair back on two legs. "Look, Chief," he said patiently. "We need the judges and Marybeth is a plus we can't pass up." He gestured toward the door. "Hell, didn't you hear Frank's wife a minute ago? She's seen Marybeth on television, on one of those talk shows. The woman's practically a star! She'd draw all kinds of free publicity."

"I don't care."

Joe dropped his chair to all four legs and tossed his hands up in the air then down to his thighs. "Fine! Then you call Penny Harris at the newspaper and talk her into publicizing the cook-off." He pushed himself to his feet and tugged his cap on his head. "And while you're at it, you might as well ask her to be one of the judges, 'cause you know damn good and well once she gets a whiff of this, she's going to want to take charge."

Joe stomped from the kitchen of the firehouse, leaving Gunner alone at the table.

Slowly, Gunner stood and started gathering cups. *Penny Harris.* God help him. Of all the people to have to ask a favor of, she was the only one he dreaded more than Marybeth Morley. The last time he'd asked for Penny's help, she'd trailed him like a bloodhound for a month, trying to pressure him into asking her out. She needed a father for her child and a man to warm her bed, and made no secret of the fact she thought Gunner Keith was the perfect man for the job.

Personally, he wasn't interested in either one of the positions.

He dropped the cups in the sink and rued the day he'd kicked in Marybeth Morley's door. But the fire department needed the Jaws of Life, he reminded himself. His steps leaden, he crossed back to the table and pulled the phone to his lap as he sat back down. He lifted the receiver, started to dial, then hit the plunger, disconnecting the call.

To hell with Joe, he told himself, slamming the receiver back on the base. Equipment or no equipment, he wasn't obligating himself to any woman. Not Penny Harris and sure as hell not Marybeth Morley.

Five

Joe pressed the doorbell and felt the first nigglings of doubt. There'd be hell to pay when Gunner found out what he'd done. He knew his friend well enough to dread the inevitable confrontation, but was convinced he was doing the right thing.

He shook off the uneasy feeling just as the door swung wide. The little girl stood in front of him.

"Hi," he said, and grinned.

She smiled back. "Hi." She tilted her head and looked at him, staring curiously. "You're one of the firemen, aren't you?"

He hunkered down in front of her. "Yeah, I am." He extended his hand. "I'm Joe Dugan."

Very grown-up, she shook his hand. "Miranda Marissa Morley."

"It's nice to meet you, Miranda Marissa Morley."

She put a hand over her mouth and giggled. "You can just call me Miranda."

He stood, understanding why Gunner was so crazy about the kid. "And you can call me Joe. Is your mom at home, Miranda?"

"Yes. Just a minute and I'll get her."

She left him standing at the front door while she raced off.

Shuffling from one foot to the other, he ran a hand across the door facing. The last time he'd seen it, it had been in splinters. Gunner had done a good job repairing it.

"Yes?"

He glanced up to find Marybeth standing opposite him. He tugged off his cap and stretched out a hand. "Ms. Morley? I'm Joe Dugan from the fire department."

Marybeth remembered him only too well. The last time she'd seen him, she'd been standing half-dressed in her kitchen and he'd ogled her like she was his next meal. "Yes, I remember you, Joe."

He patted the door facing. "Gunner did a good job repairing this."

"He didn't do it. Mr. Peters did. Gunner repaired the lock."

"Oh."

Wondering why on earth the man was there, she asked, "Are you here to check up on him?"

"No, ma'am. I need a favor."

She waved a hand toward the back of the house. "I'm sorry, but at the moment I'm in the middle of—"

"It won't take long," he said.

"But I'm—"

"Five minutes. I promise." The smile he offered her would charm the skin off a snake—or the clothes off a woman's back. Because she knew this, Marybeth had no fear of him.

"Oh, all right," she said, giving in. "But you'll have to talk while I work."

Joe closed the door and followed her down the hall, silently congratulating himself on getting this far.

In the kitchen, she positioned herself behind a center island and gestured for him to take a seat at the breakfast bar. She slapped an inch-thick strip of raw steak onto a cutting board. "What's the favor?" she asked as she picked up a meat cleaver and began to whack at the meat.

Joe watched her agitated movements, remembering Gunner's words. *One minute she's sweet as sugar and the next she's flying off in a rage.* Nervously he cleared his throat, thinking he could get this done in less than five minutes. "The fire department is sponsoring a chili cook-off to raise funds to buy some needed equipment." When she didn't so much as lift a brow, he raised his voice to make sure she heard him over the pounding noise. "We were wondering if maybe you'd consider being one of the judges?"

Without looking up, Marybeth flipped the meat over and continued whacking away. "Who is *we?*"

"Well, me and the boys at the station."

She glanced up, her eyes narrowing. "Did Gunner put you up to this?"

"No, as a matter of fact, he doesn't even know I'm here."

Marybeth digested that bit of information. For some reason it depressed her. She hadn't seen or heard from Gunner since the night he'd taken Miranda and her to dinner. And she'd wanted to. Obviously he didn't share her feelings. "When's the cook-off?" she asked on a sigh.

"Two weeks. It'll be on a Saturday afternoon and—" The meat flipped again and the cleaver came down, splattering blood across the bar. "What in the hell are you doing?"

Marybeth paused and looked up. "I'm working on a new recipe."

"For what? Beef pancakes?"

Marybeth glanced at the pulverized piece of steak in front of her and couldn't help laughing. "No. Stroganoff."

Joe curled his nose. "If you were thinking of asking me to dinner, I think I'll pass."

Tossing back her head, Marybeth laughed, too, the first good one she'd had in nearly a week. She laid the meat cleaver aside and picked up a cup towel to wipe her hands. She crossed to the breakfast bar and propped her elbows on the bar and her chin on her hands. The smile she offered Joe was open and friendly. "I think I like you, Joe Dugan. Now tell me again about this chili cook-off."

Gospel music floated from speakers concealed in the corners of the tarp shading the booth. Three women in choir robes swayed, their heads bowed, humming an accompaniment to the soulful song. A pulpit stood to the left of a black cast-iron pot of steaming chili and in front of it paced a man wearing a cheap polyester suit, waving a Bible over his head. His hair was shoe-polish black, a sharp contrast to the white patent shoes on his feet. Perspiration beaded his forehead and he mopped at it with a handkerchief clutched in one hand.

His voice rose with emotion as he paraded back and forth in front of the pulpit. "Guaranteed to burn Satan himself from the souls of the damned," he was saying as Marybeth stopped in front of his booth. "One taste of Brother Billy's Sure Fire Chili," he said, and paused, lifting his face and hands dramatically to the sky, "and the gates of Heaven itself will open up to you."

The handkerchief came down, slapping the cover of the frayed Bible and making Marybeth jump as Brother Billy whirled to face the crowd that had gathered. "Brothers and sisters," he said, his voice imploring, his tear-filled eyes pleading, "pull yourselves from the clawing fingers of that old Devil, Satan. Clean-n-se yourself. Pur-r-ge your body of all that ails you."

He dropped to his knees, hugging the Bible against his chest. "Bring sa-a-lvation to your life before it's too late. Brother Billy's Sure Fire Chili is the answer, the very *cure* to a life destined to Hell." He dropped his chin to his chest, and closed his eyes, his shoulders racked with soft sobs.

"Amen, Brother!" someone yelled from the back of the crowd, and laughter erupted.

Brother Billy lifted his head, looked straight at Marybeth and winked. The devilish gleam in his eye and in his smile made her laugh, too, and she tucked her clipboard under her arm and added her applause to the others in the crowd. Pulling the clipboard back out, she put a big star beside Brother Billy's Sure Fire Chili on her judging sheet and moved to the next booth.

Now that she was here, actually participating in the chili cook-off, she was glad she'd accepted Joe's invitation to act as a judge. She couldn't remember the last time she'd had this much fun, laughed so hard, or met so many nice people—all be they a bit bizarre.

Easing back from the crowd, she stood on tip-toe and searched the area for Miranda. She finally spotted her daughter on the wooden playground equipment, giggling and swinging with two little girls. Sighing in contentment, Marybeth once again congratulated herself on her decision to move to Terrell.

She loved the feel of this place: the small-town atmosphere, people who smiled and waved even when they didn't know you. From the sack boy at the grocery store to the postman who brought her mail. Even the man at the gas station who washed her windshield and checked her oil though the sign out front distinctly read Self Service.

But most of all, she liked the change for Miranda. Friends her age, a yard to play in, the freedom of movement and activity that the condo in Dallas hadn't offered. Marybeth sent up a silent but hopeful prayer that Miranda would respond to the changes, that she would find happiness here in her new home, contentment in the environment Marybeth hoped would foster balance in her daughter's life.

"This one gets my vote."

The whispered comment from the female judge beside her drew Marybeth's attention back to the booth. She glanced down at her clipboard and the list attached. Jack's Rattlesnake Chili. She eased forward to get a better glimpse.

Six feet and two hundred pounds of solid mountain man stirred this pot. A black Stetson rode his head and an earring made from a snake's rattle dangled from his right earlobe. He wore jeans and boots, but Marybeth couldn't take her eyes off his chest. Nothing but bare skin and curling chest hair lay beneath a snakeskin vest.

Muscles rippled across his chest and his nipples rose in twin peaks as he stirred the wooden paddle through the steaming chili. Tanned skin glistened beneath a sheen of perspiration. The sight of so much raw maleness made a shiver work its way down Marybeth's spine.

I've got to stop this, she told herself and looked away. For two years her hormones had lain dormant, sleeping, but ever since the episode with Gunner they'd been working double time and driving her crazy. At the oddest moments she'd find herself remembering Gunner's kiss, the feel of his arms, wondering what would have happened if she hadn't hit him in the stomach and ended the intimate moment.

The very idea that she would harbor such lustful thoughts alarmed her, but it was her body's response to those same thoughts that scared her the most. At the mere thought of the man, her stomach would go all soft and squishy, her hands would tremble, and the most god-awful ache would start deep inside her. She couldn't sleep, she couldn't work, she was irritable and snappish with anyone with whom she came in contact. What was wrong with her?

She stole another glance at Rattlesnake Jack. It was a mistake. Her eyes blurred and suddenly it was Gunner's chest before her, not Rattlesnake Jack's. She felt again the heat of his chest penetrating her breasts, the strength of it as he'd held her in his arms. Groaning, she closed her eyes and willed the lustful thoughts away.

"Marybeth, you're drooling."

Her eyes flipped open with a start. Joe stood beside her, leaning close, his eyes teasing, his cheek almost touching hers. Flustered, she backed away.

"And who wouldn't with all these wonderful smells tempting their taste buds?" She scribbled a notation on her clipboard, hoping to convince Joe her mind was on chili and not on a man, then tucked the board under her arm. "So when do we start tasting?"

He glanced at his watch. "About thirty minutes. Can I buy you a lemonade?"

"I need to check on Miranda first," she said, rising on tiptoe to look over his shoulder.

"She's with Gunner. I saw them a few minutes ago over by the game booths. I think she was trying to talk him into winning her a teddy bear."

Marybeth squashed the bubble of jealousy that arose. She was sick, truly sick, if she was jealous of her own daughter. At that instant her eyes met Gunner's through the crowd. His gaze moved from her to Joe then back again. A frown as dark as a thundercloud built on his face.

Jealous? Gunner? The thought put hope in her heart and a devilish gleam in her eye. She looped her arm through Joe's and grinned up at him. "So where's my lemonade?"

"Marybeth! Look what Gunner won for me!" Holding the bear by its legs, Miranda waved it above her head as she ran toward her mother and Joe. She skidded to a stop at her mother's feet. "Isn't it neat?"

"Neater than neat," Marybeth replied, and passed Joe her empty cup. Smiling, she took the bear from Miranda and smoothed the fur down his back. "What's his name?"

"I haven't given him one yet." She tipped her face up to Gunner, who had joined them. "Since you won him for me, why don't you name him?"

Gunner took the bear and held him at arm's length, studying him. After a few seconds he handed the bear back to Miranda. "Smokey," he said.

"Now that's original," Marybeth muttered under her breath. She hadn't meant for Gunner to hear the comment, but the look he shot her said he had.

"Perfect," Miranda beamed.

Joe watched the exchange and tried not to laugh. Mating was a funny thing—both in the wild and in civilization. Animals squared off nose to nose, slapping and clawing at each other, playing a little teasing game while dropping their scent and laying out their territory.

Hell, he'd played the game himself often enough to know. He'd fallen in and out of love more times than he could count and if his experience was worth anything at all, he'd swear these two had fallen hard.

They just didn't know it yet. But maybe he could give them some room to tangle and find out for themselves.

He squatted down eye-level with Miranda. "That bear looks awful thirsty. Think maybe we oughta buy him a lemonade?"

Miranda giggled and slipped her hand into Joe's. "Can I have one, too?"

"If you promise not to make a prune face."

"What's a prune face?"

"Like this." Joe wrinkled his nose and scrunched his mouth.

Miranda giggled again. "I promise."

Marybeth watched them walk away, their hands swinging between them, painfully aware of the man who remained at her side.

"You and Joe sure seem to have hit it off."

The statement threw her totally off guard and she wasn't sure how to answer. Seeking a neutral response, she said, "He's a nice man."

"Yeah, he's that." Gunner dug the toe of his boot into the dirt, chipping away at a rock embedded there. "Marybeth, I know this is none of my business, but Joe has a reputation around town."

"Oh?" she asked innocently, though she was dead certain she knew where this line of conversation was headed.

"Yeah, he's kind of a womanizer."

"Really?" she said in mock disbelief.

"Yeah. I thought I'd warn you, you being new in town and all." The rock broke free and he gave it a little nudge with his boot. "Just in case you—well, you know..."

Marybeth stepped in front of him, forcing him to look at her and not at the rock. "In case I fall for him?"

Uncomfortable with her nearness and the angry glint in her eyes, he took a step back. "Well, yeah."

"You're right," she replied, closing the gap right back up. "It isn't any of your business. But just to put your mind at rest, I can take care of myself."

Gunner put a hand to his stomach, remembering. "Yeah, I guess you can."

Holding on to her temper, Marybeth sucked in a deep breath and blew it out through her teeth. "Gunner, I don't know what it is about you, but you really tick me off. And at the moment, I need to burn off some steam."

She grabbed him by the hand and dragged him toward the game area. She passed ring tosses, floating ducks, coin tosses and dismissed them all as too tame. Physical is what she needed. Energy-sapping, sweat-producing physical. Her eyes focused on a booth at the far end sporting a target and a stack of baseballs and she took off, dragging Gunner behind her.

"Put up or shut up," she said, pushing up her sleeves.

Gunner lifted a brow, but without a word he placed a dollar on the stand and watched the vendor set three baseballs in front of Marybeth. He waved a hand, palm up, in invitation. "Let her rip."

Marybeth picked up a ball and rubbed it briskly between her hands. She eyed the target and for her own satisfaction placed an image of Gunner on the bull's-eye. Her eye on the mark, she reared back for the pitch, then lunged forward, putting all her weight behind the throw. The ball whizzed through the air and smacked the bull's-eye dead center. Lights flashed and a siren wailed.

Marybeth smiled and dusted off her hands.

Stunned, Gunner could only stare. He should have known. Anybody who could throw a punch like she had, could certainly wipe the color off a bull's-eye. "Beginner's luck," he grumbled irritably.

Wearing a smug look, Marybeth picked up the second ball. She reared back and let it fly. She was already reaching for the third ball by the time the lights flashed and the siren wailed, signaling another win.

A crowd started gathering behind him as Gunner watched her prepare for the third pitch. She stood in profile, her eyes narrowed at the target, her mouth set, her hands cradling the ball at her chest. She looked like a major league pitcher sizing up a batter.

As she wound up for the pitch, her arm came down and around and his gaze slipped to her fanny... and he forgot all about her form. The cutest little butt that had ever filled a pair of jeans twisted artfully just out of his reach. When she lunged forward for the throw, it was all he could do to keep himself from filling his hands with both cheeks.

The ball smacked home, setting the lights flashing and the siren wailing. Marybeth whirled around and threw her arms around Gunner's neck, nearly squeezing the breath out of him. "Did you see that?" she screamed, laughing and tossing back her head. "I did it! I hit the bull's-eye every time." She planted a kiss full on his mouth, then wheeled back around and slapped her hands on the counter. "What do I win?" she demanded of the vendor.

Slowly, Gunner released his breath while the man placed a rubber snake in front of Marybeth. The woman was crazy. One minute she was scratching and hissing and the next she was firing up his heater with a kiss. He didn't know whether to wring her sassy neck or pull her into his arms and kiss her senseless.

At the moment kissing her senseless held more appeal.

Stepping up beside her, he winked at the vendor behind the booth. "My money's on the lady and we have a hankerin' for that pink teddy bear hanging above your head.''

Marybeth held a hand to her stomach and puffed out her cheeks in a long breath. If she didn't eat chili again for six months, it might be too soon. The judging was over, the prizes awarded and the entrants were packing for home. In her estimation—and if the happy smiles on the volunteer firemen's faces were any indication—the cook-off had been a resounding success.

''All done?''

Marybeth glanced up to find Gunner leaning against the tree beside the judge's table, the pink teddy bear tucked under his arm. The sun was almost gone, and a ball cap shadowed his eyes, but his voice still held that easy camaraderie they'd established at the gaming booth earlier that afternoon. ''Yes, thank heavens. Got a Rolaid on you?''

Gunner chuckled. ''No.'' He glanced around. ''Where's Miranda?''

''Jennifer invited her for a sleep-over.''

Gunner already knew that, but wanted it confirmed. ''Still feel the need to blow off some steam?''

Marybeth chuckled and rubbed at her sore right shoulder. Hurling twenty-four baseballs had gone a long way in reducing her anger. ''No. I think I'm about all steamed out.''

''Good.'' He caught her hand and tugged her to her feet. '' 'Cause I feel the need for some speed. The carnival's staying open until midnight and I'm ready to give that Octopus a whirl.''

Because she wanted to, Marybeth allowed him to tug her along, her hand clutched tightly in his. The carnival stretched over the parking lot of the football stadium next to Lion's Club Park with rides appealing to all ages. As evening shadows took over, colored lights blinked on. Calliope music and barkers' voices filled the cool night air.

Together Marybeth and Gunner ducked in and out of lines, screamed and laughed their way through a haunted house, had their breath stolen on the roller coaster, and shared a quiet moment while perched at the top of the ferris wheel. At last, they reached the infamous Octopus.

"Think you're up for this?"

Marybeth watched the long arms of the Octopus snake out, twist wildly, then snap back to the center before whirling away again. A sucker for cheap thrills, she was already digging money out of her jeans' pocket. "You bet, but this one's my treat." She gave his cheek an affectionate pat. "Unless you're too chicken?"

Laughing, she raced off and climbed into an empty car. Gunner scooted in beside her and clipped the safety belt around their waists. Her fingers closed over the bar just as the car started to move.

Sluggishly at first, as if in slow motion, the Octopus arm snaked out, reached the limit of its extension, and spun the car attached to its tentacle slowly three revolutions before dragging it back. Gradually the speed picked up until the car was literally hurled from the center like a comet out of space. The force of the whirling motion threw Marybeth against the back of the car. Excitement pumped through her veins, making her laugh and scream with each new twist.

Then suddenly it hit her. About two pounds of chili started dancing a tango in her stomach. Her smile slowly faded and she swallowed hard, fighting back the nausea.

"Gunner," she whispered. "Make them stop." But the wind whipping at her face stole her voice. *Oh, Lord, please don't let me throw up,* she thought desperately. Letting go of the bar with one hand, she grabbed at Gunner's elbow. Without looking at her, he laughed and reached over and squeezed her hand.

She swallowed again and pressed her head back against the protective screen behind her and curled her fingers tightly around the bar. On and on the car whirled, twisting and turning, churning that chili to a froth in her stomach. Finally she couldn't stand it anymore. "Gunner! I'm going to be sick!" she screamed.

Marybeth stabbed the toothbrush in her mouth and swiped a tear from her cheek. She'd never been so humiliated in her life. Blustering about how brave she was, then throwing up all over Gunner. She groaned, remembering.

A soft tap sounded at the bathroom door. "Marybeth? You all right?"

Wincing, she dragged the toothbrush from her mouth and spit the flavored paste into the sink. "Yes. I'm fine," she replied, then muttered under her breath, "Except for my ego."

"Are you decent?"

Her eyes widened in alarm. Surely he wasn't coming in? "Just a second," she called. She leaned over the sink to look in the mirror. Her hair was plastered to her head as a result of the shower she'd taken and her face was still deathly white. She pinched her cheeks, trying to put color back into them.

Before she could do more, the door eased open and Gunner's head appeared in the opening. His eyes met hers in the vanity mirror and held as he stepped further into the dressing room. "Are you feeling better?"

Marybeth tried hard to breathe. She was feeling better—or at least she had been before he'd appeared. Fresh from the shower, he faced her in the mirror wearing only jeans and a smile. His hair was slicked straight back and wet tendrils curled at his neck and at his ears. His feet were bare and—Lord—so was his chest. She'd never seen him without a shirt . . . but she'd imagined. And her imagination hadn't done justice to the real thing.

Like Rattlesnake Jack's, his chest was covered in a fine layer of dark curling hair. Anchored on pads of muscle, rosy nipples peeked from beneath the dark fuzz. Her gaze slid down further and she discovered a new meaning for the word washboard. His ribs were the only definition in a stomach as flat and rigid as a board. At the waist of his jeans, her breath locked in her throat. One snap remained open, creating an interesting V that pointed downward.

Her stomach started doing that squishy thing and her hands began to tremble. She felt what little bit of color she'd pinched back into her face drain away. Gunner was beside her as she sagged against the sink.

"Marybeth, are you okay?" he asked in concern.

Fighting back the weakness, she could only whisper, "Yes, I'm fine."

He guided her to the vanity stool and pushed her down, kneeling beside her as he brushed damp hair away from her face. "You don't look fine. You look sick."

Insulted, she pushed angrily at his hand. "Well, thanks!"

Sighing in frustration, he said, "I didn't mean that the way it sounded."

"And just exactly how did you mean it?"

He dipped his head, his shoulders sagging. When he lifted his face, the look of remorse in his eyes pulled at her heart. "I don't know why, but for some reason, every time I open my mouth around you, whatever I say comes out backward." He sighed again and took her hand in his, the pad of his thumb moving to massage her palm. "What I meant was, you're still pale and you seem unusually weak. Are you sure you feel okay?"

The heat from his thumb was slowly burning a hole in Marybeth's hand. Nervously, she wet her lips. "I'm fine. Really," she said, and pulled her hand away. She tried to stand, to escape the smothering sensation his nearness created, but he pushed her back down. Reluctant to meet his gaze, she plucked at the hem of her robe.

"No, you're not," he said, and caught her fidgeting hand in his. Noticing the tremble in her fingers, he pressed two fingers against her wrist. While he measured her pulse, he mentally began to take stock of her symptoms: cold, clammy hands, paleness, unusual weakness and now a thready pulse. Everything added up to shock. "We need to get you into bed, and elevate your feet. Warm you up."

"What I need," she said, jerking her hand from his, "is to get away from you." She stood, but in her haste to put distance between them she bumped against him. He lost his balance and sat down hard on the floor. He stared after her as she paced away.

She picked up a brush from the vanity and jerked it through her hair, sending droplets of water flying. "*You're* my problem."

"Me? What did I do?" he asked innocently.

"Nothing," she said, wheeling to face him again. "Absolutely nothing. And *that* is what is driving me crazy." She slammed the brush down on the vanity and marched back across the room to stand over him. "Every time I get near you, I get this stupid squishy feeling in my stomach and start feeling feverish and light-headed."

"And that's my fault?"

"Yes, it's your fault!" She stooped to shove her face to within inches of his. "I haven't been with a man in over two years!" she fairly screamed at him. "And I hadn't given it a moment's worry until I met you."

Watching her, he curved his lips in a slow smile. "Really?"

"Yes, really. And I don't like this feeling one—"

She was falling before she realized he'd even moved. When she landed, one of his arms was beneath her knees and the other roped her waist. His mouth came down covering hers, biting off any other hope of communication.

Six

Her breath stolen, she lifted her hands to his chest to push him away. She didn't want him to kiss her. She wanted him to go home, to leave her alone, to get out of her life and stay out. Forever. Since the day he'd knocked down her door, she'd lost control of everything, including her emotions.

But when her fingers met the warmth of his chest, she forgot all about pushing. Her arms grew weak and she curled her fingers in the nest of chest hair and clung.

Maybe she didn't want him to leave just yet. Maybe she wanted him to make love with her. And that's what was driving her crazy, she realized. The maybes.

She was used to being in control, knowing exactly what she wanted and working toward that goal in a logical, systematic progression. Just like working out a new recipe. Adding a little here, deleting a little there, working until she achieved the exact blend of ingredients to produce a perfect combination.

Marybeth liked control. More, she needed it. And at the moment she could feel it spinning away.

"Gunner, you've got to stop," she gasped.

His lips moved to her ear and nibbled at her lobe. Stopping was the furthest thing from his mind. "Give me two good reasons."

She closed her eyes against the seductive play, struggling to keep the passion from clouding her thoughts. "One, I'm not ready for this. Two, I don't think you're ready for this, either."

He shifted under her, letting her hips sink down between his thighs. "I'm more than ready."

She felt the bulge of manhood against her hip and nearly swallowed her tongue. "Physically, yes," she said in agreement.

"What else is required?"

Marybeth had to think hard on that one—which was difficult since he was setting fires at her neck with his lips. The heat was burning away all rational thought. She batted his face away so she could concentrate, but his lips returned, his warm breath fanning the flames higher.

"I don't know," she said, finally giving in to the sheer pleasure of it all. She turned in his arms and lifted her face to his. "And I don't care," she added in a whisper before claiming his lips with her own.

Surprised by the sudden change from reluctance to aggression, Gunner locked his arms around her, taking her with him as she slowly pushed him back against the thick carpeting. Plush wool buffed his back while silk chafed his chest. She shifted over him, seeking a more comfortable position, but her lips never once left his. The movement tugged the robe higher on her leg and he smoothed his hand up the tanned skin, his fingertips brushing her inner thigh, drawing a low moan from Marybeth.

He pushed the robe higher still until the fabric lay bunched at her waist and his hands cupped her from behind. The fit was perfect—from the way she filled his hands to the way her body molded to his. Somehow he'd known it would be this way between them. Why, he wasn't sure. Certainly there was nothing to base it on, for from the moment they'd met, they'd done nothing except butt heads.

But they weren't butting heads now, he thought with a sigh. Maybe a nose now and then, but no heads. And he didn't intend to do or to say anything to ruin this moment.

He smoothed his hands up and around her, easing his fingers between their bodies until he found the knot in her robe's belt. Untying it, he pushed the soft folds away until her breasts lay bare against his chest. The sensation of skin against skin nearly snapped his control.

"God, Marybeth," he moaned, wrapping his arms around her, squeezing her to him as he rolled to reverse their positions. He held himself above her, his hands braced on either side of her face. In her eyes, he saw the same desire that burned in his.

His body throbbed with need, already demanding release. He wanted to take her then and knew by the passionate glaze in her eyes, the thud of her heart slamming against his, he could. But he wouldn't give in to that need. He wanted to go slow, to give her pleasure as she'd never known with any other man.

His eyes skimmed lower, from her eyes to her lips, down the smooth column of her neck to her breasts. He'd been right the first time, he decided as he shifted to his side and cupped one small globe in his hand. She really didn't have much upstairs.

The nipple peaked and hardened beneath his thumb and he couldn't resist taking it into his mouth. The texture was coarse velvet, the taste, strawberry sweet. He felt more than saw the arch of her body as he drew on the rosy bud... but he heard the soft groan emitting from low in her throat and knew what she yearned for.

He slid his hand down, his touch feather-light, gently massaging his way down the smooth plain of her stomach, intent on nothing but pleasing her. Skin as soft as satin warmed beneath his touch. At the V of her legs, he laid his palm across her mound and gently cupped her femininity. Her body arched violently beneath the weight of his hand. He didn't move. Instead he simply held her, letting the need build within her as he laved first one breast then the other with his tongue before shifting to press his lips just above her navel.

Marybeth grabbed at his hair. "Gunner, please," she begged.

"Please what?"

"Make love to me," she whispered.

"I am making love to you," he said, nipping once more at her stomach before raising his head to look at her.

"No," she cried, her head rocking back and forth against the carpet in denial. "I want you inside me."

He reached for the button of his jeans, but Marybeth's fingers were already there, tugging and fumbling until each one was free. She strained, fighting the stiff denim down over his hips. Pushing her hands away, he kicked the jeans free then lowered himself over her, once again bracing a hand on either side of her face. She grabbed at his hips, guiding him, urging him toward her.

The initial contact had her tensing and arching away. Fearing he'd hurt her, Gunner started to pull back, but then her hips rose to meet him, taking him in, wrapping him in her warmth. The flush on her cheeks, the fever-bright eyes told him she was close and he wanted to give her everything and take nothing for himself. He remained poised above her, unmoving, and waited.

He watched her face as her body tensed beneath him, her fingers digging into his buttocks, her eyes growing wide. The pulsations of her climax throbbed around him. He stayed perfectly still as pleasure slowly smoothed the tension from her face.

"I hate you," she whispered, her breathing labored.

Fearing he'd done something wrong, Gunner asked, "Why?"

"You didn't even move. You just…you just…and still it— Well, I—" She laughed, covering her cheeks with her hands. Her embarrassment eased his concern. "That's never happened to me before," she said, her gaze searching his. "How did you do that?"

"I wanted the pleasure to be all yours." His lips curved in a half-smile. "Now how about we try for one together?"

Her arms fell limply to her sides. "I can't. I'm dead."

He lowered his mouth to hers, taking her lips in a kiss that sipped away at her breath. "Luckily, I'm a paramedic and know C.P.R." Her lips parted beneath his, and he teased her with his tongue, stroking and probing...promising. Then he began to move within her, slowly at first, gradually increasing speed until her body responded, her hips picking up the age-old rhythm and racing with him.

Desire built, clawing within him like something wild and untamed, fighting at the constraints that held it. On and on he moved until perspiration misted his chest and his back. Blood thundered through his veins until he thought he'd surely explode.

"Now, Marybeth," he groaned, and rose on his knees above her to clutch her hips between his hands.

"Yes," she whispered. "Oh, God, yes."

He held her against him as wave after wave of shudders racked his body, draining the very life from him. Slowly he lowered her hips to the floor and collapsed against her.

His breath heaved warm and fast at her ear. "And I thought you were dead."

She was in her bed, but really didn't know how she'd gotten there. Her last conscious thought had been of lying on the bathroom floor, her limbs tangled with Gunner's, her cheek nestled at his neck. She'd succumbed to the lethargy following their love-making and fallen asleep to the sound of his even breathing.

She stretched her foot out, found Gunner's and curled her toes around his. Sleepy-eyed, but smiling, he rolled toward her and tugged her to his side. Satisfied, she snuggled against him.

"Is it morning?" he asked, his voice husky.

"No, not yet."

"What are you doing awake?"

"I was trying to remember how I got to my bed."

"I carried you." He squeezed her tighter against him, his lips finding the sensitive skin at her temple. "I never was one for sleeping on floors."

A loud beeping sound had Marybeth bolting upright. Gunner was out of the bed, charging for the bathroom while in the distance a siren ripped through the night. He returned, tugging his pager from the waist of his jeans. He plopped down on the side of the bed and switched on the lamp. Marybeth blinked at the sudden brightness.

"Structure fire," he said almost to himself as he read the message on the miniature screen. The address flashing was in a neighborhood he was familiar with. Old wood-frame houses shoved up so close together, when one person spit someone in the next house wiped his eye. If one residence caught fire, at least two others were sure to flame. And in each one, a minimum of three kids.

He stood, jerking on his jeans. "I've got to go." He stooped to peck a kiss on her cheek, but hit only air. She reached for him, but he was already turning away.

He disappeared into the bathroom and came out hopping as he tugged on first one boot then the other. "I'll call you tomorrow," he tossed over his shoulder when he reached the bedroom door.

And then he was gone.

Marybeth lay back against the headboard, pulling the sheet to her chin. The change in him from the moment the pager had gone off was almost scary. One minute he'd been lying in bed, all cuddled up, whispering to her in the darkness. Then boom! He was up and running, jerking on clothes, his face and shoulders tensed, his forehead plowed in deep furrows.

She listened as his truck engine roared to life and the tires squealed as he sped down the drive. In the distance, the siren continued its mournful wailing.

A shiver worked its way down her spine.

"Oh, hi, Gunner!" Miranda wriggled her way up onto the bar stool, covering the phone's mouthpiece with her hand. "Marybeth," she whispered, "it's Gunner."

Marybeth nodded and smiled at her daughter, then turned her back to hide the hurt. Three days had passed without a word from him. When he'd left in the middle of the night, he'd promised to call the next day. He hadn't. And now? She heaved a frustrated breath before turning to sit on the bar stool opposite Miranda.

"Yep, I sleep with Smokey every night." Miranda crossed her legs, swinging one bare foot daintily to and fro. "How about you? Who do you sleep with?"

The question—though innocent—had Marybeth sucking in a horrified breath. At Miranda's burst of laughter, Marybeth's eyes narrowed and she wondered what Gunner had said that could possibly be that funny.

"Yes, she's here. Just a minute and I'll get her." Miranda covered the mouthpiece again and stretched the receiver out to her mother. "He wants to talk to you," she whispered in excitement.

Marybeth took the phone and forced a smile. "Thank you, Miranda." Placing the receiver at her ear, she said, "Hello?"

"Hello, Marybeth."

His voice was low, seductive, and had her heart slamming against her chest. But she wouldn't give him the pleasure of knowing how just the sound of his voice affected her. To ensure this, she threw a few ice cubes into her reply. "Well, hello."

"About the other night..." he began, then stopped to clear his throat.

"Yes?" she prompted.

"I apologize for not calling sooner."

Though his silence had hurt more than she cared to admit, she replied, "No apology necessary."

Silence prevailed for a full five seconds. Finally, Marybeth asked, "Was there something else?"

"Well, uh, yeah, there was," he said slowly. "I had promised Miranda she could come out and ride Midnight and I was wondering if y'all had plans for today?"

"Y'all as in me and Miranda?"

At the sound of her name, Miranda's eyes brightened and she leaned across the bar expectantly.

"Well, yeah," Gunner said, sounding puzzled by her question. "I thought we could ride for a while, then I could throw some burgers on the grill and y'all could eat dinner with me out here."

Marybeth wanted to say "Thank you, but no thank you" being as how he hadn't found the time to call her in three days, but the excited look on Miranda's face wouldn't allow her that pleasure. "That's very kind of you, Gunner," she said, trying to work up the proper enthusiasm. "Miranda would enjoy that very much."

"Good. I'll pick y'all up about two-thirty. See you then."

Marybeth stretched to place the receiver on the wall unit beside the bar.

"I would enjoy what very much?" Miranda asked, barely able to contain her excitement.

"Gunner has invited us out to ride horses this afternoon."

Miranda shot up in the air, waving her hands above her head. "Yippee!" When her feet hit the floor she danced around the room, singing and laughing. Then she froze, whipping around to face her mother, her hands clapped at her cheeks. "I don't have a thing to wear!"

Marybeth rolled her eyes. "Jeans and tennis shoes will do nicely."

"Just a little while longer, Gunner. Please?" Miranda begged.

Gunner reined in his horse at the gate to the corral, and glanced back over his shoulder, chuckling. "For the nineteenth time, Miranda, no. Two hours is long enough. You're probably going to be so sore tomorrow as it is, you won't be able to walk."

He swung a leg over the saddle horn and slid to the ground, keeping the reins in his hand. Leading his own horse, he walked back to catch hold of Midnight's bridle. "Remember which side to dismount from?" he asked Miranda.

"Yes. The left." Reluctantly she kicked free of the stirrup, and slipped to the ground. He had to bite back a smile when he saw the pout on her face. He'd forgotten how much joy a pony could give a little girl.

Holding out the pony's reins, he offered gently, "Why don't you walk Midnight around and cool him off a bit before we unsaddle him?"

Miranda's face brightened immediately. "Can I?"

"Sure. Just stay within sight of the barn. Holler if you need me. I'll be unsaddling your mother's and my horses."

Marybeth heard this exchange from the relative safety—if not comfort—of her horse's back. Unlike Miranda, for her the ride couldn't end soon enough. Even though Gunner had assured her the mare she rode was as gentle as a lamb, her hands ached from the tight grip she'd held on the reins.

But that ache was nothing compared to the one in her rear.

"Need any help?"

Still miffed with him, she replied coolly, "No, I can manage." Gritting her teeth, she gathered the courage to swing a leg over the horse's wide rump and slowly eased herself down. When her feet hit solid ground, needles of pain shot up her legs. Her knees buckled and she sagged against the horse's side, groaning.

Gunner was at her side, his hand at her elbow. "You okay?"

No, she wasn't okay! She was hot, sweaty, and ached in places she hadn't thought possible to ache. She tried to stand, but her legs refused to cooperate. She fought back the bubble of hysteria that rose in her throat. "I can't straighten my legs."

"For God's sake, Marybeth. Why didn't you say something earlier?" He slung one of her arms around his shoulder and, supporting her weight, guided her to a bale of hay beside the corral.

His impatience coupled with her own weakness humiliated and infuriated her. "I didn't say anything," she replied tersely, "because I didn't know I couldn't stand until I tried.'' She jerked free of him and then slowed her movements to ease down on the bale of hay. Folding her arms at her breasts, she turned away, refusing to look at him.

At the far end of the pasture, she saw Miranda petting Midnight's neck while the pony grazed peacefully at her side. Thankfully her daughter was out of earshot, but well within sight.

''Are you mad at me or what?''

Tears burned behind her eyes. Furiously she blinked them back. ''And what would I have to be mad at you about?'' she asked, her tone brusque and unforgiving.

''Hell, I don't know,'' he said, snatching off his cap and slapping it against his thigh. ''But you haven't said two words to me since I picked y'all up.''

Suddenly she whirled to face him, tears glistening from her eyes in the bright sunshine. ''You could have called me.''

''I did call you!''

''Yes, today. But you said you'd call three days ago. And considering . . .''

For a moment Gunner stared, waiting for her to finish, wondering what was behind this anger. Then it hit him. *Slam-bam-thank-you-ma'am*. That's what she thought that night with her had meant to him. And all because he'd failed to call when he'd promised.

Sighing, he hunkered down in front of her. He lifted her foot to his knee and gently began to massage her calf. ''I'm sorry, Marybeth, but I didn't have the chance to call.'' He paused, his hands growing still a moment before starting to knead at her calf again. ''That's not exactly true. But close.

"The call I answered the night I was with you was on a structure just south of town. A water heater exploded. The house went up like dry kindling and spread to three other houses before we could get it under control. While we were in the midst of fighting that one, a grass fire broke out on the Paris farm. A railroad runs through their property and when the six o'clock train ran through a spark off the track set the pasture on fire. The wind helped it along, destroying about twenty-five acres of hayfield before we were able to turn it."

His hands moved higher, over her knee to her thigh. "That kept me busy until about seven that night and then I went home. I could have called you then—I should have—but I was so blamed tired I crashed." He cocked his head to look up at her, a lopsided grin chipping away at one corner of his mouth. "You see, I didn't get much rest the night before." Seeing the set of her lips, the hurt in her eyes, he sighed, then resumed the massage.

"Then about 5:00 a.m. my pager went off. This time an accident out on Interstate 20. A church bus full of campers and an eighteen-wheeler. We worked about five hours on that one. Then—"

Marybeth reached out a hand, putting a fingertip to his lips, hushing him and drawing his gaze to hers. "You don't have to say any more." Pulling her hand back, she plucked at a piece of straw on the bale, too ashamed to look him in the eye. "I'm sorry, Gunner. You must think I'm a self-centered brat."

He caught her hand and pulled it back to his lips. "No, I think I'm an awfully lucky man." He pressed a kiss to the palm of her hand, then licked it. Fire raced up her arm at the brief contact. "And please

don't think that night with you wasn't special, 'cause
it was.''

"Gunner?"

"Hmm?" he murmured, his lips already moving to
the sensitive skin on the underside of her wrist.

"Why do we always fight?"

"Hell if I know. But maybe it's because we're passionate people," he suggested before tugging her from
the bale to his lap. "But I'd rather make love than war.
How 'bout you?"

Gunner slipped the bridle from Midnight's head and
gave the pony a slap on the rump as she trotted away
to join the other horses in the pasture. He stooped to
slide the bar onto the gate, locking it.

A dog raced around the side of the barn, barking
furiously. A dirty beige with rust-colored freckles
scattered along his tangled coat, he looked big enough
and mean enough to eat a person whole. Miranda hit
Marybeth's side and stuck like a fly on tar paper.

"Rusty, heel." At Gunner's command, the dog
hushed and slunk to his side. Gunner put out a hand
and the dog licked it, his tail kicking up dust as it
swiped the ground. Gunner motioned for Miranda to
join him. She inched toward him, taking a wide girth
around the dog.

"Miranda, I want you to meet Rusty. Rusty, Miranda. Shake, boy." The dog lifted a paw, and cautiously Miranda took it. A smile slowly built on her
face.

"Is he yours?"

"I inherited him." Gunner leaned over and picked
up a stick from the ground. He threw it and the dog
raced off, then returned seconds later carrying the

stick in his mouth. "Here," Gunner said, offering her the stick. "You try."

Miranda threw the stick. Rusty raced off, and Miranda took off after him, squealing in delight.

"Miran—"

Gunner caught Marybeth by the arm when she would have stopped her. "Let her go. She'll be fine. Rusty'll look out for her." His hand slipped to hers. "Let's go start the grill."

In the distance, Marybeth could hear Rusty's barking and Miranda's squeals of laughter. The sound comforted her, but it was Gunner's assurance of her daughter's safety that allowed her to leave Miranda behind while she followed Gunner to the house.

They strolled, their hands locked and swinging between them, down a path beaten through time and frequent travelings. The distance to the house was short, but ample for Marybeth to get a clear picture of his home. She wasn't sure what she'd expected, but nothing had prepared her for what met her eye.

Late afternoon sun glanced off the structure, warming the stone exterior to a honeyed hue. Azaleas lined the front of the house, and though they weren't in bloom, Marybeth could well imagine the dramatic display in the spring. Circumventing the front, Gunner led her to a flagstone walk that wound around the side of the house and they followed it to a patio around back.

The same native stone framed the patio in a low wall. Pots of rose moss were scattered about, vibrant spots of color against a backdrop of green pastures and blue sky. At the opening to the patio, Gunner dropped her hand and moved to the grill, digging a book of matches from his pocket.

Marybeth hung back, taking it all in. Just beyond the patio, shaded by two giant oaks, a hammock swung lazily in the breeze and to the left a rope swing dangled from a branch as thick as a telephone pole. She could almost see a child swinging there, feet kicking at the bright green leaves overhead, as the swing was pushed higher and higher, the trill of laughter filling the air.

This wasn't a bachelor pad, a place a single man would choose to hang his hat. The carefully manicured lawn, the flowers, the rambling ranch house. This was a home.

It suddenly occurred to her that she knew absolutely nothing about Gunner Keith. Did he live with his parents? Was he divorced? Did he have children as the pony and the swing hinted? Her curiosity aroused, she glanced over at him. His back was to her, his shoulders moving easily beneath his Western-cut shirt as he arranged the coals on the bottom of the grill. The wind plucked at the dark curls brushing his collar and rearranged the part in his hair.

Unaware he was being watched, he picked up the book of matches and struck one, cupping a hand around the flame as he guided it to the coals. His shirt sleeves were cuffed nearly to his elbow, revealing muscled arms and black hair curling over tanned skin.

His hands were strong, confident in their movements and Marybeth felt heat crawl up her neck as she remembered the way those same hands had moved on her. The match touched the coals and flames leaped up, chasing Gunner's hand away. He dropped the match onto the coals and turned, holding out a hand to Marybeth in invitation.

"Want to check out the hammock while we wait for the coals to get hot?"

Her voice wouldn't work. She tried to say yes, but she couldn't seem to push the word beyond the desire clogging her throat. Her feet wouldn't work, either. They seemed to have grown to the flagstones beneath her feet. Gunner came to her, catching her elbows lightly in his hands.

"Legs still bothering you?"

The excuse he offered was so much easier than the truth. She seized it, nodding her head, her gaze fixed on his, while a tremulous smile built at her lips.

"Well, we can take care of that." He scooped her up, nearly stealing her breath, and strode for the hammock and the shade. Carefully balancing the roped bed with one knee, he laid her down, then eased down beside her, setting the hammock beneath them swaying. Lifting her head slightly, he tucked his arm beneath it and pulled her against his side. Sighing, he cupped his opposite hand beneath his head and closed his eyes.

Sunlight filtered through the leaves, hypnotizing Marybeth as the hammock swung rhythmically to and fro. But the questions raised after seeing his home wouldn't go away.

"Gunner?"

"Hmm?"

"Do you live alone?"

He opened one eye to peer at her. "Yeah, why?"

She shrugged the shoulder pressed against his chest and plucked at a piece of straw that clung to his shirt. "This place just seems made for children. The pony, the swing..."

The flash of tension shot through him so quickly Marybeth wouldn't even have been aware it had happened if their bodies hadn't been pressed so close.

"This was the house I grew up in. I inherited it."

She would have asked more, but he closed his eyes and settled his head back in the crook of his arm. Though he looked relaxed, frown lines remained between his brows. Marybeth smoothed them away with a gentle touch. Without opening his eyes, Gunner caught her hand in his and pulled it to his chest. The rhythmic beat of his heart and the warmth of his hand on hers gave her a sense of peace as nothing she'd ever known.

Nature created a symphony of sound around them. Birds twittered overhead, a light breeze rustled through the branches. In the distance, as her eyelids grew too heavy to hold open, she could just make out the sound of Rusty's barking and an occasional squeal of laughter from Miranda.

Smiling her contentment, she snuggled against the warmth and comfort of Gunner's side.

Seven

Not asleep and not awake, Marybeth was caught in that wonderful dreamland of peacefulness that lay somewhere between the two. Dappled sunshine warmed her face and a light breeze cooled her skin. The distant sound of Rusty's barking mingled with the constant hum of insects buzzing overhead and tugged her closer to wakefulness. She listened, waiting for the answering sound of Miranda's laughter. When she didn't hear it, she sat up, blinking back the webs of lethargy.

The barking grew stronger and stronger and she watched as Rusty topped the small knoll behind the house, charging at her like a member of the light brigade. Miranda was nowhere in sight.

Nervously she touched a hand to Gunner's shoulder. "Gunner?"

Instantly awake, he was up and swinging out of the hammock. "What?"

Before Marybeth could voice her concern, Rusty was there, sliding to a stop a good ten feet from Gunner. He barked three times in rapid succession, wheeled, raced off about five feet, then turned and barked again, looking at Gunner expectantly.

"Miranda," Gunner murmured and took off running.

Marybeth felt the blood drain from her face. Fighting free of the burdensome hammock, she ran after Gunner. He disappeared over the knoll and when Marybeth reached the spot, she stopped, her breath hitching in her chest as she tried to determine which way he'd gone. She caught a glimpse of his red shirt just before he ducked into a stand of pecan trees on the far side of the meadow.

She raced down the small incline, her heart slamming against her chest. *Oh, God, please let Miranda be all right,* she prayed fervently as she fairly flew across the field. Twice she tripped on the uneven ground and fell, scrambling back to her feet, fear clogging her throat as she stumbled on toward the spot she'd seen Gunner last.

When she reached the stand of pecans, she found they were simply a border around a small clearing. Within the secluded spot was a small cemetery enclosed by a white picket fence. Wildflowers covered the ground and a child's playhouse stood in the center of the blanket of color. Two tombstones of grey marble stood tall and somber to the left of the house. To the right, a single tombstone stood alone.

The fence's gate was open and the bottom half of the playhouse's Dutch door gaped wide. Marybeth ducked under it and stopped just inside the door. Her hand went to her heart and she swallowed back the fear that had burned in her throat since the moment Rusty had appeared alone.

Gunner sat beside a small grave with Miranda on his lap, one tiny arm slung around his broad shoulders. Rusty lay sprawled on the soft ground beside them, his sides heaving, saliva dripping from his lolling tongue.

"Who is Laura?" she heard Miranda ask in a soft voice.

"My sister."

"It says," she said, pointing to the pink granite stone at the head of the grave, " 'Budded on Earth to bloom in Heaven.' " She lifted her face to Gunner's. "What does that mean?"

"It means she was born on earth but now she lives in heaven."

"Is she an angel?"

"Yes, she is."

Marybeth heard the tremble of emotion in his voice and fought back tears.

"Why is this house here?"

"This was her playhouse. I built it for her sixth birthday. She used to spend hours playing in it. After she died, I moved it out here and placed it over her grave."

"Why?"

"Because I thought it would please her."

Miranda glanced around at the miniature windows draped with gingham faded by weather and time, then back at the pink stone, her fingers curling around Gunner's neck. "I'm sure it does."

"Miranda?"

At the sound of her mother's voice, Miranda twisted around in Gunner's arms to peer over his shoulder. "Hi, Marybeth. This is Gunner's sister's playhouse. He built it for her. Isn't it wonderful?"

Slowly, Marybeth crossed the short distance to kneel behind the two. "Yes, it is, darling," she whispered, reaching to tuck a lock of hair behind her daughter's ear. She added the weight of her arm to Gunner's shoulder and lightly squeezed. Their gazes met and she saw the sadness in his eyes. "And you are, too," she added, giving his shoulder another squeeze.

Miranda lounged on the floor in front of the television with one arm locked around Rusty's neck, the other cupped behind her head. The dog raised his head at the sound of Marybeth's step, at once protective and alert. When he saw her, he lowered his head back down between his paws, the look in his eyes once again indulgent. Smiling at the tender scene, Marybeth tucked the bread basket under her arm and picked up the last plate from the table and carried it to the kitchen.

Gunner stood at the sink, a dish towel tucked at his waist for an apron, his wrists limp at the edge of the sink, staring out the window to the darkness beyond. Ever since they'd returned to the house, he'd seemed unusually quiet and withdrawn. She suspected Miranda's questions had dredged up long-forgotten memories and opened wounds that hadn't had time to heal.

After placing the plate and basket on the counter, she touched a hand to the center of his back and leaned around him. "Want me to finish up?"

He shook his head. "No," he said, and dipped his hands back into the sudsy water. "I'm almost done."

"Want to talk?"

He cocked his head to look at her, his forehead plowed into a frown. "About what?"

"Whatever's troubling you."

Picking up the last of the plates, he plunged them into the water, averting his eyes. "Nothing's troubling me."

Marybeth took a finger and pressed it to the worry lines above his nose. "Then why the frown?"

Sighing, he took a step back and bent at the waist, planting his forearms on the edge of the sink and his forehead in the crook of his elbow. "Because it still hurts," he murmured, then cocked his head to look at her. "After ten years, it still hurts."

The tears glistening in his eyes had Marybeth reaching for him. She wrapped her arms around him and guided his cheek to hers. She felt the shudder that passed through him and felt the warmth of the single tear that squeezed between their pressed cheeks.

"Tell me about her," she whispered in encouragement, sensing that he needed to talk even though he'd denied it.

A minute passed, maybe two, in silence while Marybeth waited, continuing to hold him. Water dripped from the sink faucet in a steady splat-splat-splat, hitting the sudsy water and bursting the translucent bubbles one by one. The rhythm matched that of Gunner's controlled breathing at her ear.

"She was only six," he said finally, his voice husky with emotion. "She and my stepmother, Phyllis, were here alone." Another shudder passed through him, and Marybeth rubbed her hand up and down his back in a soothing motion, as she would to comfort Miranda.

He took a deep breath and pulled away from her, turning to stare out the window again. His fingers found the edge of the sink and curled around it, squeezing until his knuckles turned white while the memories built. "My mother died when I was fifteen and Dad married Phyllis shortly after her death. Laura was born two years later. She was my half sister. A cute kid, full of spunk. A lot like Miranda. We all spoiled her rotten.

"While I was in college, Dad was killed in a freak hunting accident. Phyllis never got over it. To deal with the grief, she started drinking. I didn't know at first. She hid her habit pretty well. Then, after I graduated, I moved back here to take care of the farm until Phyllis could decide what she wanted to do with the place. That's when I discovered she was an alcoholic.

"The night they died, I'd gone out with some friends. Phyllis drank herself into a stupor and fell asleep in bed with a lighted cigarette." Marybeth heard the bitterness in his voice and the guilt, as well. "She was burned beyond recognition. This end of the house—" he said, turning with a wave of his hand "—was pretty much destroyed. The other wing—Laura's and my rooms—suffered only smoke and water damage."

"And Laura?"

"She died of smoke inhalation."

She would have liked to touch him. To take him in her arms again and comfort him. But he folded his arms across his chest and leaned back against the counter, his aloof stance holding her at bay. Words were all she could offer. "I'm so sorry, Gunner. It must have been very difficult for you."

His gaze dropped to the toes of his boots and remained fixed there. "Yeah, it was. When I found Laura, she was lying in her bed. She looked like she was asleep. So peaceful." He heaved a deep breath, stuffing his hands down hard into his jeans pockets. "When I picked her up, I realized she was dead." He twisted his upper body to stare out the window again. The muscles in his jaw worked as he fought for control. "At first I thought I'd sell the place, but when it came right down to it, I couldn't. Mom and Dad were buried here. And Laura."

"Your parents are the two graves beside the playhouse?"

"Yeah. Dad always said he wanted to be buried beside Mother."

"And the one on the other side?"

"That's Phyllis. I put Laura between her and Dad."

He shrugged and pushed away from the counter, seemingly distancing himself from the memories as easily as he'd distanced himself from the counter. She wondered if this was his defense mechanism. If he didn't allow himself to think about it, he wouldn't feel the pain.

He caught her hand and pulled her along behind him. "Most of the remodeling I did myself." At the end of the hall, he shouldered open a door and flipped on the overhead light. "The fire started here. The master bedroom."

The story of the devastating night still fresh in her mind, Marybeth peeked around him, expecting to see charred ruins.

Instead she was greeted with starkness. Bare walls painted a softy putty color and carpeting of a similar shade. The only relief to the blandness came from a tangle of sheets and quilts covering a king-size waterbed.

"I gutted the room and enlarged it," he said, leading her to French doors. He pushed one open and stepped out onto a patio, moonlight spilling across his uplifted face. "Sometimes, when it's not too hot, I sleep with the doors open. I like the night air and the peaceful sounds." He stood staring out into the velvety darkness, his thoughts as distant to Marybeth as the galaxies that spanned the night sky.

After what seemed an eternity, he turned and rested a hip against the low stone wall, once again folding his arms at his chest. The moon formed a crown above his head, the stars, jewels that twinkled and shimmered before her eyes. "Thanks for listening, Marybeth," he said, his voice low and husky. "I didn't realize how badly I needed to talk."

Sleep wouldn't come. Marybeth flipped over again, to her back this time, and stared at the shadowed ceiling above. Moonlight filtered through lace drapes at her bedroom window and tatted fancy patterns on the pale peach ceiling. She tried to focus on the intricate designs, tracing and counting, waiting for sleep to come. But her mind kept reaching back, replaying the past Gunner had shared with her.

That he'd suffered was obvious. And who wouldn't under similar circumstances? In the span of ten short years he'd lost his mother, his father, his stepmother, and his half-sister. Quite a load for anyone to bear alone. Just look at what the loss of her father alone had done to Miranda. Marybeth dealt almost daily with the psychological trauma of that one event.

To deal with her own loss of her husband, Mary-beth had joined a grief support group. The strength she drew from them was what had helped heal her and gave her the foundation, the stamina, to help Miranda. The stages of grief she'd learned from the group's leader were so stark they were easily recognized. Denial, anger, depression, and finally—hopefully someday, she prayed for Miranda—acceptance.

The one stage obvious in Gunner's demeanor was anger. The bitterness she'd heard in his voice told her that but it was the guilt she'd heard, as well, that was keeping her awake. He blamed himself for Laura's and Phyllis's deaths, and that just wasn't healthy to Marybeth's way of thinking.

Somehow, some way, she hoped to help him absolve that guilt.

Exhausted and cranky from the few hours' sleep she'd been able to claim, Marybeth said, "Mother, why don't you go boss Angela around for a while?"

Helene picked up a pair of jeans from the floor and gave them a hard shake. "I'm not bossing you around. I'm giving you motherly advice." She stepped around Marybeth to pull a hanger from the closet. Draping the denim over the hanger, she added, "Besides, your sister lives too far away."

"How far is too far?" Marybeth mumbled as she snatched the hanger from her mother and disappeared into the closet, mentally giving serious consideration to moving again. This time farther away.

"What did you say, dear?"

"Nothing," Marybeth said as she stepped from the closet and sank down onto the vanity stool in her dressing room. "Trust me, Mother. I can handle my own life."

"I know you can, dear, but—"

Marybeth had known the "but" was coming and just managed to keep from tearing at her hair.

"—Miranda needs a father. A man's influence in her life. And you don't seem to be doing anything to find one for her."

"Miranda is doing just fine."

Helene halted her inspection of Marybeth's collection of perfume bottles long enough to look down her nose at her daughter. "Of course she is." She picked up a bottle and unscrewed the lid. "But she still needs a father. And you need a man." Waving the bottle under her nose, she breathed deeply of the scent. Her shoulders sagged and her eyelids fluttered. "Heavenly," she breathed. "Maybe if you wear a little of this next time you're with Gunner, he'd—"

Marybeth jerked the bottle from her mother's hand and slammed it down on the counter. Amber liquid splashed across the marble countertop, filling the room with its heavy floral scent. "I don't need perfume to woo Gunner."

"Are you saying you're already involved with him?"

Sensing she'd just fallen into her mother's clever trap, Marybeth tightened her lips. "I didn't say any such thing."

Helene smiled knowingly. "You don't have to. The blush on your cheeks says it all." She patted one beneath a manicured hand. "Maybe Miranda will have a man in her life, after all."

The idea obviously pleased her, for Helene smiled smugly as she recapped the bottle and pulled a tissue from a brass container to wipe up the spill. "I think I'll plan a little trip for Miranda and I, so you and Gunner can have some time alone."

"Mother, please don't interfere."

Helene twisted around, placing four fingers at her breasts. "Me? Interfere? I just want to spend some time with my granddaughter, that's all."

Picking up one of Joe's favorite phrases, Marybeth mumbled, "Like hell."

Marybeth heard the truck in the drive and leaned across her desk to peer out the window just in time to see Gunner step from it and Miranda skip down the sidewalk to greet him. He reached down and swung her up above his head, making her laugh.

"How's my favorite girl?" she heard him ask as he lowered her to the ground.

"Fine. Did you come to play with me?"

He squatted down on his heels, putting himself at eye level with her. "Well, maybe. I need to talk to your mom first, though. Is she home?"

Marybeth ducked away from the window just as Miranda lifted a finger to point in her direction. "Yeah, she's in her office working on an article. Want me to get her for you?"

Gunner ruffled her hair, then stood. "No, that's okay. I'll find her."

Marybeth began scrambling through papers, trying to look as if she was busy, though Lord knew she wasn't. She hadn't been able to do a thing since he'd called earlier to tell her he was going to drop by. She heard the faint creak of the front door opening, then a thud when it closed. His footsteps sounded heavy on the hardwood floors as he crossed the hall to her office.

Then silence.

Her back to the open door, she waited, her ear tuned to the slightest movement, her skin crawling on her back because she knew he was watching her. Impatiently she pushed at her bangs, frowning at the papers in front of her, wishing he'd hurry and say something.

"You sure are cute when you work."

The breath sagged out of her and she dropped her forehead to her palm. "Gunner. You startled me," she lied.

He crossed to stand behind her, dipping his head over her shoulder to peer out the open window in front of her desk. "Nice view." Marybeth followed his gaze and nearly groaned. Parked right outside the window in perfect view of her desk was his truck. Miranda sat on the sidewalk at the edge of the drive, picking petals from a daisy, her lips, painted a ruby red, mouthing "He loves me . . . he loves me not."

"Okay, so I knew you were here," she admitted reluctantly as she bunched the papers into a neater pile.

His head turned and his lips found the curve of her neck. "You're even cuter when you're embarrassed."

She started to push him away, then instead wrapped her arms around his neck and pulled him to her lap. "I didn't want to appear overanxious."

"You? Overanxious? Never." He nuzzled her neck, tickling her and making her smile. "Am I too heavy?" he asked when she shifted beneath him.

"Yes, you weigh a ton." When he started to get up, she linked her arms at his waist and held on. "But a nice ton.'' She wrinkled her nose and buried it at his neck, sniffing. "Yuck. You smell like smoke."

"Do I?" He caught the collar of his shirt and pulled it to his nose. "I guess I do. That's why I'm late. Another grass fire. I didn't take the time to shower and clean up before I left the station."

"That's okay, but I didn't tell Miranda you were coming just in case something came up. She doesn't accept disappointment very well."

"And her mother does?"

Reminded of the major pout she'd thrown when he hadn't called for three days, Marybeth winced. "Ouch! That one hurt."

Gunner chuckled and eased off her lap. He swiveled to prop a hip against the desk opposite her. "The reason I called is to ask your permission about something before I discussed it with Miranda."

Curious, Marybeth lifted a brow. "Oh, and what would that be?"

"Well, she seemed to get such a kick out of Laura's playhouse, I thought maybe if you didn't mind, I could build one for her."

Marybeth's mouth dropped open in surprise. "Gunner, how sweet!"

"I don't know how sweet it is, but I've got a couple of sacks of concrete in the back of the truck. We could pour the foundation today if it's all right with you."

"Well, of course it's okay with me." She glanced at the clutter of papers on her desk, gently gnawing at her lip while trying to decide if she'd have time to finish the article later and wishing she'd worked on it instead of pacing her office waiting for his arrival.

Gunner noticed the look. "I don't expect you to help. I know you've got things to do." He pushed away from the desk and stooped to drop a kiss on her cheek. "I'll take Miranda around back with me."

Responsibility held Marybeth in her chair as she listened to the front door slam shut and Gunner's shout for Miranda. She leaned toward the open window again and watched as Gunner dropped the tailgate and swung a sack of concrete onto his shoulder. He scraped a tool belt off the bed of the truck and handed it to Miranda. Weighted down by the burdensome load, Miranda struggled to keep up with his long stride, chatting excitedly as they headed for the back. The two disappeared and Marybeth flopped back down on her chair, feeling left out and lonely.

"Damn work, anyway," she muttered as she snatched up the pile of papers and began to sort through them.

Two more trips were made to the truck. One to unload a stack of lumber and haul it to the backyard. A second for a wheelbarrow, which Gunner swung Miranda into after dropping it to the drive. The bumpy ride drew squeals of childish laughter and the sound floated through the window and pulled Marybeth's mouth down further into a frustrated frown. She wanted to play, not work. She wanted to share this time with Miranda and Gunner, not be stuck in her office alone with a deadline breathing down her neck.

Determined to finish so she could play, too, she stuffed a piece of typing paper into her typewriter and tugged her notes and recipes on planning and preparing a romantic dinner for two to the edge of her desk. Blocking out the enticing sound of hammering and murmured conversation coming from the backyard, she focused her concentration on the notes in front of her.

Nearly two hours later she pushed back her chair and rose, arching her back, her hands pressed at the curve of her spine, and groaned. The article was finished and faxed to the food editor at *Southern Living*, the notes filed, and her responsibilities complete. Now she could play.

Grabbing her empty coffee cup, she hurried to the kitchen. Juanita stood before the kitchen table, a stack of clean towels in a heap in front of her, her hands smoothing and folding but her eyes glued to the scene beyond the bay window. A smile tugged at her lips.

Marybeth walked up behind her and peered over her shoulder. "What's going on?"

"Oh, Señora Morley," Juanita said, catching a fluffy towel at her mouth and chuckling. "They are so funny. Miranda, she is in the way more than she helps, but Señor Gunner is so patient. A moment ago he asked her to squirt water from the hose into the wheelbarrow while he stirred up the cement. The little scamp, she turned the water full in his face, soaking his head and his shirt." She laughed out loud and gave the towel a snap, folding it neatly into halves and then into thirds. "He didn't fuss or complain. He just took the hose and soaked her good from head to toe." She laid the towel on the stack of folded ones and picked up another from the pile. "They are like two little puppies, rolling and playing. So cute," she said, chuckling again.

Anxious to be a part of the fun, Marybeth headed for the back door. "Hey, you two," she called from the back porch. "Need some help?"

Gunner and Miranda glanced up at the same moment from their kneeling position over the foundation. Water dripped from their hair and spiked their eyelashes. Miranda's T-shirt was plastered to her thin chest, leaving a perfect impression of her training bra. Fortunately today she'd left out the wads of tissue she usually stuffed it with. Marybeth hated to think what shape the soggy tissue would have taken on if it had been in place.

Gunner's shirt hung by its collar from the handle of the wheelbarrow. His chest was bare and sunlight captured the moisture clinging to the hair there, turning it to shimmering diamonds.

A smile slowly spread across his face. "You're just in time for the dedication."

"Dedication?" she repeated as she crossed the short distance to where they worked.

Gunner made one last swipe with the trowel, then dragged it across the board framing the foundation, scraping the last dregs of cement from the metal tool. "Yep. The dedication. Take your shoe off," he instructed, sitting down on the grass to tug off his own boot and sock. Miranda followed suit and placed her bright pink tennis shoe next to his boot, then rose to stand beside him, both of them standing and waiting on Marybeth.

Not sure what was going on, Marybeth shook her head but willingly kicked off a sandal. "Okay, now what?"

Gunner placed his bare foot on the wet cement, lightly pressed, then lifted it off, leaving a perfect impression of five toes and a heel. He motioned Marybeth to stand beside him. She hoisted a foot, holding on to Gunner's shoulder for balance and placed it next to his print. The cement was wet and cold and sucked at her foot as she pressed down, oozing gray mud between her toes. Wrinkling her nose at the strange sensation, she lifted her foot. Five toes and a heel, smaller and ever so much more feminine, appeared beside Gunner's print.

Next came Miranda. She stepped between Marybeth and Gunner and clutched at their hands as she pressed her tiny foot next to her mother's impression. She squealed in delight at the sucking noise her foot made when she drew it away.

Three prints. Graduating from large to small. Marybeth felt the tightening of emotion in her chest and didn't even try to suppress it. Man, woman, and child. Father, mother, daughter. The circle of life complete.

"Now what?" Miranda asked, looking up at Gunner.

"We need a stick," he said, glancing around the manicured lawn and finding nothing that would do the job.

"I had a Popsicle earlier. Will that work?" Miranda asked helpfully.

"Yeah."

She skipped off and returned with a flat stick, stained strawberry red. Gunner dug a hand into his jeans pocket and withdrew a pocketknife. Hunkering down at the side of the foundation, he whittled one end of the stick to a sharp point. He knelt and scratched *Gunner* into the still wet cement beneath his footprint, then passed the stick to Marybeth. She knelt and did the same, then passed the stick to Miranda, whose childish scrawl was almost as big as the impression of her foot. Miranda passed the stick back to Gunner, who scratched in the date, then stood and dusted off his hands.

They all stood, staring, each silent, harboring their own private thoughts. Marybeth slipped her hand into Gunner's and leaned her head against his shoulder, grateful to him for giving this special gift to Miranda.

"What next?" Miranda asked, impatient for the house to be finished.

Gunner slipped his hand from Marybeth's and draped it around her shoulder, pulling her close. She looked up at him and found the same tender smile in his eyes she'd learned to love. "The cement has to set for a couple of days, then we can start on the walls. All that's left for today is cleanup."

"Cleanup?" Miranda echoed in dismay.

"Yes, ma'am. Cleanup. You get the hose and fill the wheelbarrow with water while I gather up the tools. A carpenter always takes care of his tools." He bent and retrieved the trowel from the grass while Miranda dragged her feet to the outside faucet to turn on the water.

"What can I do?" Marybeth asked, planting her hands at her hips, wanting to help, too.

"You can give me a kiss."

Marybeth gave a surreptitious glance Miranda's way, not certain if her daughter was prepared to see her mother share such an intimacy with another man. Miranda was squirting water into the wheelbarrow, her actions as well as her expression indicating that she didn't think cleaning up was nearly as much fun as working on the playhouse.

Sensing Marybeth's uncertainties, Gunner said softly, "I think she can handle seeing her mother kiss a man."

She snapped her head around to stare at Gunner, surprised that he'd all but read her thoughts. "How can you be so sure?"

He dropped the trowel and caught her elbows in his hands, tugging her toward him. "I'm not. But she's going to have to deal with it sometime."

His lips came down, moist and cool, his half-smile and a night's growth of beard tickling her lips. Marybeth's resistance melted into nothingness.

"Hey!" Miranda called indignantly. "How come I'm doing all the work?"

Gunner turned his face skyward, chuckling low in his throat, his hands still cupping Marybeth's elbows. "See, I told you," he murmured, and rubbed his nose against hers. He yelled over her shoulder to Miranda, "You just make sure you keep that water in the wheelbarrow, young lady. I've already had one shower today." He turned his gaze back to Marybeth. "Now, where were we?"

Eight

Over the next weeks, the playhouse slowly began to take shape. Marybeth watched the progress through the kitchen window while she worked on recipes for a series of magazine articles due in September.

The studs went up first, two-by-four pine, yellowed with rosin and with a few dark knotholes scattered about. Miniature windows were framed in—two, one on the east and one on the west side of the house—and a door that Miranda insisted must be Dutch just like Laura's. The whole thing looked like a wooden skeleton to Marybeth's way of thinking, and for its purpose, she supposed it was.

While Marybeth measured, stirred and tasted in her air-conditioned kitchen, Gunner hammered, sawed and sweated under a broiling sun. Miranda passed nails and generally got in the way. But Gunner never once complained or lost his composure. With a patience that Marybeth envied, he answered her endless questions and guided her unskilled hands when she insisted on manning the saw or hammering a nail.

The sight of the two of them working together did something to Marybeth. She couldn't so much as glance out the window without stopping whatever she was doing and staring while her insides went all syrupy and warm. Marybeth knew she was a softy, a sucker for any emotional display. Anyone who cried during a television commercial for Hallmark cards had to be! But there was something about seeing the two of them together that made her yearn for things she knew she had no business yearning and dreaming things she had no right to dream.

A father for Miranda.

She wanted to blame her mother for ever planting that thought in her head, but she couldn't. Miranda did need a father. Though Marybeth had tried her darnedest after Tom's death to fill the holes his passing had left in Miranda's life, her attempts were inadequate. A little girl had needs that a mother simply couldn't fill, no matter how hard she tried.

A mother could kiss a scraped knee and make it better or sew an arm back on a ragdoll, but she couldn't give a bear hug like a daddy—the kind that swallowed you up and filled you up at the same time. She couldn't call her daughter "princess" and make the child feel that same special radiance, that same bond of love that surged if the words had come from her father. Nor could she chase away a bad dream in the darkest moments of night and make her daughter feel as safe and protected as when her father handled that duty.

But Gunner could, even if he wasn't Miranda's natural father. Marybeth could see it every time Miranda looked up at him or mentioned his name. Her eyes would brighten and the biggest smile would bloom on her face. She adored the man, and he was obviously as smitten as she.

The playhouse wasn't the only that thing grew over the weeks. A relationship that included the three of them—Gunner, Marybeth and Miranda—had grown, as well. His time off from the fire department was split between his farm and his responsibilities there and Marybeth's house. While Juanita had been away in Mexico visiting relatives, Gunner assumed her place at the dinner table, averaging at least one meal a day at Marybeth's home. His truck became a common fixture in the driveway.

His presence in their lives had wrought a change in Miranda, subtle but monumental. She hadn't raided Marybeth's closet or vanity in weeks. But the biggest surprise of all was what Marybeth had found in the wastebasket one morning. Miranda's training bra. Much to Marybeth's relief, Miranda was finally beginning to act eight instead of eighteen. Marybeth knew she had Gunner to thank for the change.

Her thoughts reflective, she sighed as she shut off her mixer. Another sound, distant and mournful emerged to take over the silence. She cocked her ear, listening to the distant siren, while the muscles knotted on her shoulders and in her neck. The response was a new one. She'd never paid a minute's notice to sirens in the past, but now she'd learned to distinguish the difference in sound from a police car and an ambulance to that of the fire truck. And every time she heard the fire siren her thoughts flew to Gunner.

Marybeth couldn't help worrying about him. Not just for his safety, but for the obsession he seemed to have for his job. Not a fire alarm was raised that he didn't personally respond to. Marybeth wasn't sure of his job description, but surely the city didn't expect him to oversee each and every fire. It seemed as if he thought if he wasn't there, the outcome of the emergency wouldn't be the same. She couldn't help wondering if this obsession didn't in some way tie in with Phyllis's and Laura's deaths.

She sighed again and picked up the dishcloth to wipe up the spatters of chocolate from the countertop. Gunner would be late again. And Miranda was already pacing the front porch anxiously awaiting his arrival so they could start the roof on her playhouse.

She crooked her neck to peer out the kitchen window to check on Miranda. Her daughter stood at the edge of the drive, staring off into the distance, held spellbound by the mournful wail of the siren. After the sound died away, Miranda turned, kicking dejectedly at the pebbles on the driveway as she scuffed toward the backyard. Marybeth knew by her daughter's actions that Miranda was as aware as she was that Gunner wasn't coming. At least not for a while.

Empathetic to her feelings, Marybeth hurried to the back door. "Miranda!" she called.

Miranda turned, her mouth turned down in the saddest sad face Marybeth had seen in a while. "What?"

"Want to help me ice the cake?"

Miranda kicked at a pebble, her hesitation indicating she'd rather be putting the roof on her playhouse with Gunner than icing some dumb old cake. "Yeah, I guess," she finally said.

Marybeth held open the door while Miranda brushed past. Forcing a smile for her daughter's benefit, Marybeth tied an apron around Miranda's waist. "I'll bet when Gunner arrives he'll be starving and he'll eat half this cake."

Miranda climbed up onto a bar stool and dropped a cheek to her palm, her expression desolate, while she lifted the spoon from the icing, watching the chocolate stretch like taffy from bowl to spoon. "If he comes," she muttered doubtfully.

Marybeth turned the first layer out on a cake plate and pushed it to Miranda's elbow. "He'll be here before you know it." Taking the spoon from her daughter's hand, she replaced it with a metal spatula. "Okay," she said cheerfully. "Start spreading."

Miranda dropped the spatula into the icing and lifted it piled high with thick, creamy chocolate. She slapped it onto the cake and dragged it across its top. Marybeth winced as flecks of cake rolled up under the metal edge. Catching Miranda's hand, she instructed as she guided, "Lighter hand, sweetheart, or there won't be any cake left to eat."

Globs of chocolate passed between the bowl and the cake without a word from Miranda. Marybeth added the second layer then turned toward the sink.

"Marybeth?"

"Hmm?"

"Why does Gunner work all the time?"

Surprised by the question, Marybeth hesitated a second before dipping the empty cake pan into the sink of sudsy water. "He doesn't work *all* the time, sweetheart," she answered as she scrubbed. "But I suppose because he's the fire chief he feels he should be there if they need him."

"Why? There's lots of other firemen."

Why, indeed? Marybeth wondered in agreement. The thought was one she had puzzled over herself many times before. She withdrew the pan from the water and caught up the cup towel to dry it. Sunshine streamed in the kitchen window behind her, hitting the shiny aluminum and bouncing off to dance on the ceiling as she rotated the pan in her hands. "I don't know, Miranda," she finally said. "I guess that's just the way he is."

A tapping sound at the back door had Miranda and Marybeth both turning. Gunner's nose and mouth were pressed against the window, distorting his face into a comical mask.

Miranda was off the bar stool and racing to throw open the door. "Gunner! You're here!"

He held out his arms shoulder high and looked down his front to his boots. "Yep. It's me, all right," he confirmed. Dropping his hands to tousle her hair, he grinned at Miranda. "Sorry I'm late, but we had a call. False alarm." He stepped across the threshold, sniffing. "Umm. What smells so good?"

Miranda closed the door and skipped to catch up with him, exhibiting more energy than she'd displayed since the alarm had sounded a half hour before. "Chocolate cake. I iced it. Want a piece?" she asked, crawling up on the bar stool and patting the seat next to her.

"Only if you've got a big glass of milk to go with it."

Marybeth couldn't help smiling as she listened to their banter. Miranda wasn't the only one who'd changed since that fateful day the fire department had kicked in her door. Gunner had changed, as well. A

side of his personality had surfaced that she'd never
suspected existed. He teased and laughed and seemed
ever so much more relaxed.

She stepped up beside him and slung an arm around
his shoulder. "Drink up. I have a feeling you're going
to need the fuel for energy. Miranda's got your afternoon planned for you."

Gunner lifted a brow, cocking his head toward
Miranda. "Oh? And what have you got in store for me
today?"

Embarrassed, Miranda replied, "Oh, Gunner. You
know. You said we could put the roof on my house
today."

"I did?"

"You know you did. Don't you remember?"

"Seems like I do recall saying that." He sagged his
shoulders, letting his hands drop limply between his
knees. "But I'm so weak from hunger, I'm not sure I
have the strength to work today."

Miranda was off the stool and yanking open the refrigerator door. "Get a plate, Marybeth," she ordered. She flung the milk jug at the bar and raced for
the cabinet. Yanking out a drawer to use as a stepping
stool, she climbed up to grab a glass from the cupboard. "And a knife," she added as she shoved the
glass in front of Gunner. Then she whirled again to tug
open a drawer. Silverware rattled as she dug for a fork.
Finding one, she slapped it beside the plate and
climbed back up onto the bar stool.

She took the knife from her mother's hand and cut
a generous wedge of cake and carefully levered it onto
Gunner's plate. Her mission complete, she took a deep
breath and folded her hands between pressed-together
knees. "Now you can eat."

Biting back a smile, Gunner looked at the huge chunk of cake in front of him. "Well, thanks, Miranda." He picked up the fork and sank it into the moist cake. He paused, the fork in midair, and wrinkled his brow thoughtfully. "Seems like I brought something for you."

Miranda leaned against his elbow, looking up at him expectantly. "You did?"

He puckered his lips. "Yeah, I'm almost sure I did. I believe I threw it in the back of the truck, but dang if I can remember what it was."

Miranda was off the stool again. "Can I go look?" she asked, hopping up and down at his side.

"Yeah, but be careful."

The back door slammed and Marybeth angled a hip onto the stool Miranda had just vacated. She touched a hand to his forearm. "Gunner, you don't have to bring her things. You'll spoil her."

He shoveled the cake into his mouth and closed his eyes, sighing as the chocolate icing melted in his mouth. Among other things, Marybeth was one hell of a cook. "Little girls were made for spoiling," he said after he'd swallowed. He laid the fork on the edge of the plate and swiveled on the stool until his knees bumped hers.

Eyes as soft and warm as the smudge of chocolate clinging to the corner of his mouth met Marybeth's. "Big girls were, too," he murmured before touching his lips to hers.

His lips were cool and moist against hers and oh so comforting. Less than twenty-four hours had passed since she'd seen him last, yet she'd missed him. Her heart filled and tears misted her eyes. How could she miss someone whom she saw almost daily?

Unable to resist, she laced her hands behind his neck and swished her tongue to the spot of chocolate she'd seen at the corner of his mouth. She licked it away, then raked her tongue along his teeth, depositing it there.

She felt the vibration of a groan coming from deep in his throat and smiled against his lips. "Good?" she asked softly as she drew away.

His eyes were closed and his wrists dangled limply from his knees. "Better than good," he said, letting his shoulders drop on a sigh. He flipped open his eyes and smiled. "Can I have another taste?"

Marybeth picked up the fork and sliced off another piece. Raising it to his lips, she smiled in return. "As much as you like."

He caught her wrist in his hand, guiding the fork away from his mouth. "Good. 'Cause I'm starving." He dipped his mouth over hers again, sipping at her breath, savoring the flavor of chocolate that still clung to her tongue. One hand still at her wrist, he moved the other to her waist, then to her thigh. Finding the hem of her oversized shirt, he slipped his hand beneath it and trailed his fingers up until he found her breast.

Filling her mouth with his warm breath, he cupped the bare mound and rubbed his thumb across the nipple, feeling it bud to life.

The back door flew open and slammed against the wall. "Is it really for me?" Miranda asked, gasping for breath.

His back to the door, blocking Miranda's view, Gunner inconspicuously slipped his hand from Marybeth's breast to her knee. He squeezed, sending her a look full of promises for later. "Yep, it's for you," he said, turning to Miranda. "Think you can use it?"

"Sure I can!" She spun, calling over her shoulder, "Marybeth, come see."

Marybeth started to rise, but Gunner's hand remained at her knee, holding her in place.

"What?" she asked, curiosity and just plain happiness tugging at one corner of her mouth.

He pecked a kiss on her lips, then grinned. "Miranda have any plans for tonight?"

"None that I know of. Why?"

He shrugged one shoulder. "I'm off duty until tomorrow at six. Just thought maybe if she was planning a sleep-over or something with a friend, you and I could..." His voice drifted off and he rubbed at the side of his nose as he looked down to check the shine on his boots.

Marybeth swore she could see a blush coloring his cheeks. "We could what?" she prodded mischievously.

He chuckled, then looked up at her over his brows. "Maybe we could plan a sleep-over at my place?"

"Marybeth, hurry!" Miranda called from outside. "You've *got* to see this."

The urge to tell Miranda to cool it rose, but she squelched it and instead smiled an apology to Gunner as she slipped from the bar stool. "Unfortunately she doesn't have plans. Perhaps another night."

She hadn't taken one full step before Miranda screamed impatiently, "Marybeth!"

Closing her eyes, Marybeth fumbled for Gunner's hand and squeezed as she slowly counted to ten. When she opened them, Gunner was staring at her curiously.

"It's my name," she told him. "Sometimes I think if I hear her call me Marybeth one more time I'll scream. Counting to ten helps."

"Couldn't you just tell her not to call you that anymore?"

Marybeth snorted as she shook her head. "If only it were that easy." She caught his hand and tugged him from the stool. "Hurry, before she calls me again."

With Gunner beside her, Marybeth approached the truck and leaned over the tailgate to look inside. A child-size rocker and a table and two chairs filled the bed of the truck. Miranda was sitting in the rocker, a smile bigger than Texas splitting her face.

"Isn't it neat?" she asked.

"Y-yes, it is," Marybeth stammered, thinking of the expense. "Gunner, you shouldn't have," she whispered to him.

"They were Laura's," he said, smoothing a hand over the table's oak finish. "I though Miranda might like to have them in her playhouse."

The wistfulness in his voice and his almost reverent touch on the wood made Marybeth aware of the depth of his gift.

"Can we put them in my playhouse now?" Miranda asked in excitement.

"Best not. At least not 'till the roof's on."

Miranda rocked to her feet. "Then let's get busy!"

Gunner looked at Marybeth and shrugged. "You heard the lady. Let's get busy."

As much as she loved her daughter, Marybeth couldn't help wishing Miranda did have plans for the night. With Miranda always around, she hadn't had an opportunity to be alone with Gunner since the night of the chili cook-off. She stood at the bay window, one index finger holding the curtains back, the other worrying her bottom lip as she watched Gunner work his way down the ladder.

Above him, black roofing paper covered the sheets of plywood she'd helped him earlier hammer into place to form the roof. Below him Miranda stood waiting, Gunner's hammer in one hand and a sack of roofing nails in the other. Bundles of shingles rested between the playhouse and the ladder.

But Marybeth had eyes only for Gunner. With each step down, the muscles in his hips rotated and tightened and his calves flexed, filling the legs of his jeans. Sweat glistened on his back and dampened his hair, making it curl seductively at his neck. She swallowed hard, thinking she'd never seen a more virile sight in her life.

She heard the front door open, but ignored it.

"Marybeth?"

Without moving from her spot at the window, Marybeth called over her shoulder, "In here, Mother."

The swinging door squeaked open, then shushed close. "Why isn't the front door locked?"

"Because I'm home," Marybeth replied, her gaze still fixed on the scene outside the window.

"You should still lock the door. Anyone could walk right in and—" Helene planted her hands at her hips and frowned at Marybeth's back. "Are you listening to me?"

"Mmm-hmm."

Huffing out a frustrated breath, Helene strode to the window and snatched back the opposite curtain. "What are you looking at so—" Her eyes lighted on

Gunner. "O-h-h-h," she said in understanding, then murmured lustfully, "Get a load of those pecs."

Shocked, Marybeth dropped the curtain and whirled. "Mother!"

Helene sniffed daintily. "Well, they are to be admired." She dropped her side of the curtain and took a moment to shake out the wrinkles her fist had left in the crisp chintz fabric. "If you were smart, you'd be out there helping."

"Miranda's helping."

"Not in the way I meant," she said, arching one brow meaningfully.

Marybeth dug her fingers through her hair, barely resisting the urge to tear at it. "Good grief, Mother. All you ever think about is sex."

"Judging by the way you were hanging on that curtain, and the amount of fog on the window, I'm not the only one with sex on my mind." Waving a hand Marybeth's way, she ordered sternly, "Go pack Miranda an overnight bag. She's going home with me."

Not five minutes earlier, Marybeth had been wishing Miranda had had plans for the evening. But now she was toe-to-toe and nose-to-nose with her mother and old habits died hard. She dug in her heels. "Miranda and Gunner are working on her playhouse."

"They're nearly through. I saw Gunner gathering his tools myself." Helene folded her arms at her breasts and tapped the toe of her shoe impatiently against the tiled floor. The staccato sound drummed at Marybeth's nerves. "Well? What are you waiting for?" she demanded to know when Marybeth didn't move.

The back door slammed open, and Miranda and Gunner pushed through, preceded by a blast of hot air.

"Mamere!" Miranda squealed, and ran to throw her arms around her grandmother's waist.

Helene squeezed Miranda to her. "And how's my little princess?" she asked, smiling.

"Great! Did you see the playhouse Gunner's building for me?"

"I did!" She looked over Miranda's head to grace Gunner with a grateful smile before looking back down at her granddaughter and tipping up her chin. "How would you like to spend the night with your Mamere?"

"Tonight?"

"Yes, tonight. I pulled down that trunk from the attic with all your mother's old prom dresses. We can play dress-up."

Immediately, Miranda was on her toes spinning to her mother. "Can I, Marybeth?"

Marybeth frowned at her mother. "Gunner and Miranda were going to finish roofing the playhouse tomorrow."

Not about to let opportunity pass him by, Gunner stepped in. "It'll wait another day."

Marybeth turned her frown on him, then looked down into Miranda's expectant face.

"Please, Marybeth?" Miranda wheedled.

Marybeth huffed out a frustrated breath. She couldn't very well fight all three of them. And what was she fighting, anyway? "Oh, all right," she said, but added, leveling a stern look at her mother, "but no staying up all night watching R-rated movies and no sugar after eight o'clock. Understand?"

"Yes, ma'am," Miranda and Helene sang in unison before dashing off to pack Miranda's bag.

Overhead, fat, puffy clouds floated across a backdrop of clear blue sky. With the hammock gently swaying beneath her, Marybeth followed their slow movement through the oak tree's tangle of green leaves and crisscrossing branches. Her thoughts were as sluggish and jumbled as the clouds. Miranda. Gunner. The relationship the two shared. Woven through it all were her feelings for them both.

As Miranda's mother, she loved and cared deeply for her daughter and would never permit anything or anyone to harm her. Miranda's adoration for Gunner concerned her. It was as if the child had placed Gunner in the spot in her heart once reserved for her father. And that was the worry. Gunner wasn't her father. He was a man who had stepped into their lives and filled holes left by Tom's passing. But was his presence only temporary? If he chose to leave tomorrow or the next day, or the day after that, what would his disappearance do to Miranda? More, what would it do to her? What were her feelings for Gunner?

She loved him. The thought formed and solidified in Marybeth's mind. She did love Gunner, she realized, though this was the first time she'd actually admitted the feeling even to herself. Her love for him had grown slowly over the past weeks, nurtured by the respect he'd won from her, the warmth and concern he'd displayed both to her and Miranda.

Something brushed her ear and lazily she batted it away, clinging to her contemplations.

"Are you ignoring me?"

Dragged from her thoughts, Marybeth turned to Gunner, who lay at her side. His face was only inches from her own. She smiled slowly and cuddled closer. "Not purposely."

"You aren't upset because I encouraged Miranda to go home with your mother, are you?"

"No." She sighed deeply, and dropped her gaze, fingering a button on his shirtfront. "I really wanted her to go so we could have some time alone. It's just that mother is so bossy. Even when I agree with her, sometimes I find myself arguing the opposite side." She peeked up at him sheepishly. "Does that sound crazy?"

Gunner chuckled low in his throat. "No. Not since I've met your mother." He placed a finger beneath her chin and tipped her face up higher. "But I'm glad to know you wanted to be alone with me. You had me worried there for a minute when it looked like you weren't going to let Miranda go. We haven't had two minutes' privacy since the chili cook-off."

Remembering Miranda's unexpected entrance earlier that day when Gunner had his hand up her blouse and other times as well over the past weeks, Marybeth laughed softly. "Miranda does have a habit of popping up at the most inopportune moments."

"I think we're safe here, though, don't you?" His hand slipped to the hem of her blouse and snaked upward.

When his knuckles brushed bare skin, Marybeth shivered deliciously. "Oh, I think so."

Knowing the remainder of the afternoon and the night were theirs, their movements were lingering, their mood relaxed and mellow. There was no reason to hurry, no one to interrupt them or demand their attention.

Marybeth wrapped her arms at his waist and nestled closer, but winced when his pager, clipped at the waist of his jeans, cut into her midriff. Its presence reminded her of Miranda's question earlier that day. *Marybeth? Why does Gunner work all the time?*

Once formed, the question wouldn't go away. "Gunner?" she asked, her fingers moving to comb his hair back from his brow.

"Hmm?" His nose at her throat, his response vibrated against her skin.

"Miranda asked me a question today that I really couldn't answer."

"Oh? What's that?"

"Why do you respond to every fire alarm?"

He tensed in her arms, but quickly relaxed. "I'm the chief."

"But does the city really expect you to respond to each and every one?"

"No."

"Then why do you do it?"

Puzzled by her persistence, he pulled back to meet her gaze. "Is it important?"

"Well, yes it is."

He rolled from his back to his side and stared up at the sky, a frown knotting his brow. "I never really gave it much thought. I just go. I guess it's because I feel responsible."

"Don't you think the other guys at the station are capable of handling any emergency that arises?"

He whipped his head to the side to stare at her as if he couldn't believe she'd say such a thing. "Well, sure I do! We've got one of the best teams in the state."

"Then why do you feel *you* have to be there, too?"

He lay there a moment in silence, his gaze still resting on hers, but his eyes became glazed, unseeing, his thoughts a million miles away. Two black birds squawked at each other in the branches overhead, setting the leaves stirring as they flapped away, one in hot pursuit of the other.

Shaking his head as if to clear it, Gunner rolled to his side once again, and smiled at her. "I honestly don't know, but I'll give it some thought. Later," he added, his voice taking on a husky quality as he dipped his mouth to hers. "At the moment, I have more important matters on my mind."

Marybeth didn't want to drop the discussion—his answer was important to her—but his lips moved insistently against hers, his tongue probing and sending delicious shivers chasing down her spine. His hand found its way to her breast again, and lightly squeezed. Sensations rolled in waves down the length of her, making the secret spot between her legs ache and her bare toes curl.

The question could wait, indeed, she decided on a sigh. Her desire for Gunner couldn't. Finding the buttons on his shirt, she worked each one free until she reached the waistband of his jeans. A tug, and his shirttail dragged out. Two more buttons were undone, then his chest lay bare to her touch. She loved the coarse hair that curled around her fingertips and the strength she felt in the pads of muscle on his chest beneath her palms. There was a comfort here, something beyond description, something intrinsic but true.

In her travellings, a thumbnail raked against a turgid nipple and she felt a soft moan build in his chest to resound against her lips. Heat built, rivaling that of the late afternoon sun that continued to pulse around them. The sway of the hammock increased beneath them, spurred by their movements, its closely woven ropes chafing against their coiled bodies.

"God, Marybeth," he groaned, catching the back of her neck to press her face within the crook of his neck and shoulder. Perspiration beaded his skin and she licked at it, savoring the salty, masculine taste of him. A gentle tug on her hair and he had her face only inches from his. Heat pulsed between them, feeding the passion that burned in their eyes. "I have a water bed and an air-conditioned bedroom not twenty from here that beats the hell out of this hammock for comfort."

"Then what are we waiting for?" she demanded, laughing.

"Hell if I know," he said, and rolled to throw his legs over the side of the hammock. He stood and scooped her up into his arms.

Nine

Marybeth's arms draped at his neck and she grinned up at him. "Is this what's known as a fireman's carry?"

"No, this is."

He swung her out and up, flipping her over his shoulder as if she weighed no more than a sack of potatoes. Squealing, she grabbed at the waist of his jeans while her head dangled at the middle of his back. A bare foot grazed his groin, and if she'd doubted his level of arousal, the swelled knot of manhood bumping her toes convinced her otherwise.

Heading for the lower end of the patio, Gunner pushed open a French door and shouldered his way through, kicking the door closed behind him with his boot. Darkness swallowed them. It took a minute for Marybeth's eyes to adjust after the bright sunlight outdoors—not that she could see anything from her upside-down position but the carpet covering the floor.

Three ground-eating strides and Gunner was tumbling her onto a tangle of quilts and sheets. The water bed rolled and pitched beneath her, its water-cushioned swells a welcome delight after the coarseness of the rope hammock. Flat on her back, Marybeth watched Gunner strip off his shirt. His arms stretched behind him, his hands tugging at first one cuff then the other. The shirt slipped off his shoulders, revealing the padded muscles of his chest. Blue-rivered veins pumped up from the effort of carrying her stood out on his arms. He tossed the shirt to a corner of the room. A boot followed, quickly chased by another.

He bent again, the sight of his denim-covered buttocks and tanned back nearly stealing her breath as he ripped off first a blue sock, then a brown one. The unmatched pair sailed through the air and landed on the pile in the corner before he turned to her once again. His hands on his hips, he wore only a half-smile and his jeans. His gaze never left hers as his fingers moved to unhook one snap, then four more, until his fly gaped wide, exposing a flash of white briefs.

Catching the briefs' elastic waistband, he peeled them down along with his jeans. A foot lifted, kicked clear of the burdensome outerwear, then a second foot appeared. Grabbing his clothes in one hand, he tossed the entire lot over his shoulder. Standing naked and proud, he grinned at Marybeth.

The smile was wasted on her. She couldn't take her eyes off the dark hair that swirled down the smooth plain of his stomach to thicken in a patch from which his manhood rooted erect and stiff.

Desire clotted her throat, making swallowing impossible. Slowly she lifted her gaze to his. Brown eyes, dark with passion, yet softened by the tenderness he tried so hard to conceal, met her blue ones. He held her gaze as he moved toward the bed.

Catching her hand, he pulled her to a sitting position, then caught the hem of her blouse and shimmied it over her head. Tossing it over his shoulder, he cupped his hands around her breasts. Marybeth sagged back, closing her eyes while supporting her weight with palms buried in the tangle of sheets. Gunner followed her, bending to flick his tongue at first one nipple, then the other. His hands snaked down her sides to catch the waist of her leggings.

Weak with a need that was slowly building out of control, Marybeth let her head drop back, but found the strength to raise her hips at his gentle prodding so he could peel the tight-fitting pants from her buttocks and down her legs. They, too, joined the heap of clothes on the floor in the corner.

Then his lips were everywhere. At her throat, on her breasts, nipping at the lobe of her ear, only to disappear to surface again on the inside of her thigh. His tongue licked and prodded, heating her skin, finding the most sensitive places, driving her nearly crazy with desire.

Wanting to touch him, to share the pleasure he was giving her, she reached out. At her gentle touch, he flinched, his already sensitized body shuddering at the unexpected contact.

Catching her head between his hands, he lowered himself over her, his lips finding purchase against hers while he fitted himself between her spread legs.

"Now, Marybeth," he urged as he filled her. His hips moved against her, guiding her, leading her on a journey that had them both gasping. The bed bucked beneath them in thrashing waves that matched the fevered pace of their lovemaking. His face flushed, his head thrown back, Gunner rose to his knees, bringing her with him to straddle him as he held her pressed close to him as shudders racked his body.

"My God, Marybeth," he groaned. He tightened his arms around her and cradled her head against his chest.

Her fingers dug into his shoulders as she clung to him. Her lips found his neck and climbed upward until she reached his lips. "I love you, Gunner," she whispered against them.

The words were out before she even realized the need to voice them. But she wouldn't take them back, not now when she knew he needed to know the depth of her feelings for him.

Her declaration was met with a silence that frightened her, but the tightening of his arms around her, the gentleness with which he cradled her neck in his broad hand, drawing her to him, holding her close to his heart, told her what words couldn't. He loved her. She knew he did.

"That damn pager," Marybeth muttered as she paced the kitchen alone. Thirty minutes earlier, the thing had gone off again, waking them from a sound sleep, scaring the wits out of her and sending Gunner bolting from the house, tugging on clothes.

Mad as she was, she couldn't help stopping in the middle of the kitchen and laughing as she remembered the sight of him huddled over the pile of clothes in the corner of his bedroom, sending panties and leggings flying as he searched for his socks. One blue, one brown. The man was obviously color-blind if he couldn't even match his own socks.

But now she was alone. And for how long? The thought sobered her.

Unable to answer the question and too awake to go back to sleep, she crossed to the den and picked up the remote control for the television. Flopping down in Gunner's recliner, she switched on the set and started scanning channels. At two o'clock in the morning, the offerings were slim.

Finding an old black and white movie from the forties, she settled back to watch and wait. Gunner's distinctive scent blended with the smell of leather and teased at her senses. Turning a cheek to the aged leather, she closed her eyes and inhaled deeply. Without warning, tears burned at her eyes. Why did he have to leave, anyway? she wondered, working herself up to a good sulk. He'd told her himself that he was off until six the next afternoon. And earlier, when she'd asked him why he responded to every alarm, he hadn't even been able to answer the question.

Sniffing the tears back, she straightened and made herself focus on the television. "When he gets back we are going to discuss this obsession of his," she told the flickering screen.

Unable to concentrate on the movie, Marybeth pushed out of the chair to roam the room. The den, as the rest of the house, was sparsely decorated: a television set, a recliner, a couch and a couple of end tables. Not a single picture graced the walls.

Four doors opened onto the den. One to the kitchen, one to the entryway, and one to the backyard. The fourth, she knew, led to the other wing, the one not destroyed by the fire. Beyond the closed door lay Laura's and Gunner's childhood bedrooms. Curiosity drew Marybeth to the door, but guilt had her hesitating, her hand on the doorknob. She caught her lower lip between her teeth. Was she snooping?

Of course you're snooping, silly, she told herself. But Gunner hadn't said anything about her not entering that portion of the house. In fact, his last words to her had been "make yourself at home." And that invitation hadn't excluded this wing, had it?

Curiosity won out and she twisted the knob in her hand. The door eased open and a wedge of light from the den exposed a long, dark hall with doors opening off each side. Fumbling her hand along the wall, Marybeth found a light switch and flicked it on.

The bright light chased away some of the eeriness that followed as her companion. She tiptoed down the hall and pushed open the first door. Finding a light switch she flipped it on. The room was bare and still held the faint scent of fresh paint.

Turning off the light, she closed the door and went to the second one. Taking a deep breath, she eased it open and peeked inside. Moonlight poured through priscilla curtains and pooled on soft pink carpet. A white iron bed stood between the two windows and on either side of the headboard, a nightstand with matching lamps. Pink rosebuds covered a comforter edged with white eyelet lace.

A little girl's room. Laura's room. Feeling like an intruder, Marybeth avoided the overhead light and tiptoed into the room. She nearly jumped out of her skin when out of the corner of her eye she saw movement. She whirled, only to find her own reflection staring back at her from the mirror hanging over a nine-drawer, cherry dresser. Planting a hand over her thudding heart, she stepped toward it. Scattered along the dresser top were frames of varying sizes. Squinting in the dimness, she chose one and lifted it to let the moonlight illuminate it. Captured within the ceramic frame was a young Gunner toting a little girl on his back while both of them smiled into the camera.

This must be his half-sister, Laura, she determined. Wanting a better look, Marybeth moved to the lamp by the bed and switched it on as she sank down onto the comforter. The sudden brightness made her squint again as she lifted the picture to her face. Her breath lodged in her throat.

"My God," she breathed, shocked by the likeness. The same color hair, the same style, the same color eyes. Even the same impish grin. Laura looked enough like Miranda to be her sister.

She dropped the picture to her lap as a memory from her grief support group came singing back. Goose bumps popped up on her arms and she folded them at her waist and rubbed at them as the memory built.

Janie Cummings had been a member of the group before Marybeth had joined. She'd lost her infant daughter, Maddy, but seemed to be handling her grief really well. She'd even started keeping a friend's baby in her home while the mother worked. Not a meeting passed that Janie didn't mention the infant, bragging on her development or laughing as she shared one of the baby's antics. Occasionally she'd slip and refer to the baby as Maddy. No one thought much of it at the time; it was a natural mistake.

But then Janie missed several meetings and when the group leader called to check on her, she was told by Janie's husband the truth of what had been happening. Janie had transferred all the love and affection she'd once bestowed on her daughter to her friend's baby. She'd become obsessive about the child and when she had her in her home, she'd dress her up in Maddy's clothes and call her by her daughter's name. The game had gone on until Janie lost all sense of reality. To her, the baby was Maddy. One day when the mother came to pick up the child, Janie locked herself and the baby in the house and refused to give her back.

A shiver chased down Marybeth's spine. *No!* her mind screamed. Gunner loved Miranda. She knew he did. And he loved her for who she was, not for her resemblance to his sister. She firmed her lips, and snatched the frame from her lap as she stood. Gunner Keith was not Janie Cummings. She crossed the room and placed the frame back on the dresser, turning her back on the others, her curiosity gone. She wanted nothing more than to escape this room and the doubts it had drawn, and fervently wished she'd never even entered it. Her movements jerky, she crossed to switch off the lamp, then practically ran from the room.

Just as she reached the door leading to the den, the phone rang. Pulling the door closed behind her, she ran for the kitchen, praying it was Gunner. At the moment she needed to hear the reassuring sound of his voice to chase away the doubts her discovery had brought.

She grabbed the receiver on the third ring. "Hello?" she said breathlessly.

"Marybeth? It's Joe."

"Joe," she said in surprise as she glanced at the kitchen clock. "Is Gunner with you?"

"Uh, yeah, sort of. He had a little accident and we're at Terrell Community Hospital."

Marybeth grabbed at the wall and sagged against it, her knees nearly buckling. *Gunner, hurt? Oh, please, God, let him be all right.* She clutched the receiver tighter to her ear, forcing herself to listen.

"He's going to raise hell when he finds out I called, but I thought I better warn you before I brought him home."

"Is he hurt badly?"

"Nothing serious. They put some stitches above his eye, but he took in a lot of smoke. He's gonna have one hell of a headache for a while and not much energy. The doc wanted to keep him overnight, but you know Gunner. He wouldn't have any part of it." She heard Joe's weary sigh and could just imagine what kind of hell Gunner was raising with the doctors and nurses in the emergency room. He wasn't a man who liked coddling. "Do you think you can keep an eye on him?" Joe asked.

"Yes," Marybeth replied hurriedly without giving a moment's thought to her ability to handle his injuries. "Just get him home. I'll take care of the rest."

After hanging up the phone, Marybeth ran to the bedroom and straightened the sheets and quilts, fluffing pillows and folding back the covers in preparation for Gunner's return.

She raced to the adjoining bathroom and whipped open the medicine cabinet hanging above the sink. Joe had said he'd have a headache and she wanted to make sure there were plenty of aspirin on hand.

A can of shaving cream, deodorant, a mutilated tube of toothpaste were shoved aside in her search. Finding a bottle, she carried it with her to the kitchen. Standing on her toes, she looked out the window above the sink, watching for the glare of headlights. Minutes ticked by, feeling like years, before she saw the arc of lights as Joe swung Gunner's truck onto the drive leading to the house. A second set of headlights followed.

Marybeth yanked open the back door and ran to meet them. Joe pushed open the driver's door and the interior light exposed a sleeping Gunner, his head dropped back against the seat. A patch of gauze was taped over his left eye, the white sterile cloth nearly matching the pallor of his skin. Marybeth's hands went to her mouth.

Joe draped an arm around her shoulders and squeezed reassuringly. "Believe it or not, he looks worse than he feels." He guided her around to the other side of the truck. "They gave him something for the pain and he's pretty groggy. I'll help you get him inside and into bed."

Between them they hauled Gunner out of the truck and maneuvered him into the house and on to the bedroom, him blustering all the way about how he didn't need any help, he could walk by himself. But the dead weight Marybeth alone struggled beneath, convinced her he was as weak as a newborn kitten.

At the side of the bed, he put up a fight, but Joe ignored him and shoved him to his back on the water bed and reached for a boot. He ripped off one, then the other, exposing one blue sock and one brown. Tears welled in Marybeth's eyes at the sight. Gunner was so busy taking care of everyone else, he ignored his own needs. He needed someone to look out for him, to match his socks... to keep him safe.

Fighting back the tears, she peeled the socks from his feet while Joe worked his pants down his legs. Trading places with Joe at the side of the bed, Marybeth started freeing his shirt buttons. She couldn't help noticing the tear on his sleeve, the black soot that clung to the starched cotton, and wondered how close he'd come to death. The thought sent a shiver chasing down her spine and her already trembling fingers fumbled as she tried to tug the shirt over his shoulders. Joe's hands joined hers, rolling Gunner to first one side, then the other so Marybeth could pull the shirt free.

Gunner pushed himself to his elbows. "I've got to get to the station," he mumbled groggily.

Joe eased him back against the pillows and drew the sheet up over him. He leaned down to brush a lock of hair from Gunner's brow. "You take it easy, Chief," he murmured softly. "We'll take care of things at the station."

The love and concern behind the gesture tore at Marybeth's heart. The tie that bound these men was one she knew she'd never understand. They both stood, Marybeth and Joe, beside the bed, watching in silence for a good ten seconds before Joe breathed out a long, heavy sigh. "Looks like he's down for the count," he said in a low voice.

Marybeth slipped her hand into his and squeezed. "Thanks, Joe. I don't know what I'd do without you." She sucked in a shuddery breath as she stared at Gunner's ashen face, wondering what she'd do without this man she'd grown to love. "Can you tell me what happened?"

Joe just shook his head, his gaze still locked on Gunner's face. "We were working an apartment fire. We'd evacuated all the units and had things under control when some woman started screaming she couldn't find her son." He leaned and tucked the sheet around Gunner's shoulder. "Damn fool charged back in to look for him, knowing the roof was going to cave at any minute. He found the kid and was on his way out when it collapsed. He fell on the kid to protect him and a beam took a chunk out of his head. He crawled the rest of the way to the fire escape, dragging the kid with him."

The scene Joe described was much too vivid in Marybeth's imagination. Gunner crawling through choking smoke, his head bleeding, flames licking around him as he clutched the small child to his chest. "Is the boy all right?"

"Yeah. They're keeping him overnight. He suffered some smoke inhalation, too." He shook his head again, his gaze still locked on Gunner's face. "How many times are you going to push your luck before your number comes up, Chief?" He stood for a moment, staring, the question echoing around them, then sighed and turned away. "Guess I better go."

Marybeth followed. "Can I get you a cup of coffee?"

"Better pass. J.D.'s waiting outside to take me back to the station."

At the back door, Marybeth stopped and looked up at Joe, worry knotting her brow. "Is there anything I need to do for him? Any special instructions?"

"The doc said to wake him every two hours since he took a pretty good blow to the head. Other than that, just aspirin." He shook his head, chuckling as he pulled open the back door. "I don't envy you the job. Gunner makes a lousy patient."

Joe's warning that Gunner made a lousy patient was an understatement. Every two hours she woke him, though she wished she could have let him sleep off the effects of the smoke he'd inhaled and the drugs he'd been given for pain. Once awake, he was surly, obstinate, demanding he was strong enough to get out of bed. Fortunately he was all talk and no muscle. Still, he wore Marybeth out trying to keep him in bed.

Asleep he wasn't much better. He'd moan and clutch at his head. She soothed him with cool cloths and a soft voice, trying to ease the pain and keep his hands from ripping off the bandage and opening up the stitches. Throughout the long night and while dawn opened up the sky, Marybeth remained at his side, watching, waiting, praying. Joe's statement resounded in her mind and in her heart. *How many times are you going to push your luck before your number comes up, Chief?*

She knew Gunner's job was dangerous. She knew too how seriously he took his job. But did he carry his responsibilities beyond his own safety? Joe's comment suggested this wasn't the first time Gunner had risked his own life to save another's. What pushed him to take such risks?

Her mind drifted to Laura and Phyllis. Were they the reason behind his obsession? Did he feel that in some way he could make up for the loss of their lives by saving others? She remembered the night he'd told her about the fire that had taken their lives. He'd indicated that if he'd been there he could have prevented it. Was it guilt that made him put his own life in jeopardy, as if by saving others he could absolve himself of the lives he'd lost?

Marybeth took the cloth from his forehead and dipped it into the bowl on her lap. After squeezing out the excess water, she refolded it, leaning to stretch it from temple to temple. He sighed in his sleep and reached for the cloth as the cool moistness touched his skin.

Releasing the cloth, she caught his hand in hers and brought it to her lips. The faint smell of smoke still clung to his skin. Her heart swelled with her love for him. She couldn't let him live in the past any longer, offering his own life as a sacrifice for others. She needed him and Miranda needed him.

Tomorrow they'd talk, she decided. She had to make him understand.

Marybeth stood at the stove stirring oatmeal. Joe hadn't mentioned a restricted diet for Gunner, but she sensed that he needed something bland but filling to help him regain his strength.

Beside her, midmorning sunshine streamed through the kitchen window, its presence comforting, washing away some of the fears that had haunted her through the night. She hummed as she stirred in milk and sugar.

"Good morning."

Gunner's voice, gruff with sleep, had her turning, spoon in hand, dripping oatmeal on the floor. He stood with one hand propped high on the door facing, supporting himself, while his other hand rubbed at the coarse hairs on his chest. He was dressed in only his briefs. The bandage above his eye made the shadows beneath them appear even darker. The deep furrows on his forehead and the deep creases at the corners of his eyes told her his head still ached.

"Good morning to you, too." She dropped the spoon back into the pan and wiped her hands on the cup towel at her waist as she crossed to him. Gently she brushed the hair from his brow to inspect his bandage. "How are you feeling?"

"Like hell."

Chuckling, she looped her hands behind his waist. "You look it."

"Thanks," he muttered dryly.

"You're welcome. Want some breakfast?"

The mention of food made Gunner's stomach roll. He tightened his hold on the door facing, waiting for the nausea to pass. "Not just yet. Maybe some coffee." He took a step toward the stove, brushing Marybeth aside, intending to get the cup himself. One knee buckled. Darkness threatened and he grabbed for something to hold on to but found only air.

Marybeth was under his arm when the second knee bent. Straining under his weight, she threatened, "Don't you dare pass out on me, you big lug, or I'll never get you back to bed."

Her voice echoed through the darkness sucking at him. Although the room continued to spin, he frowned and attempted to put some starch back in his knees. "Not going to faint," he said, denying his weakness. Leaning heavily on her, he turned back toward his room. "Just need to lie down for a minute."

One hand rode the wall while the other dug into Marybeth's shoulder. He hated the weakness. More, he hated Marybeth seeing the weakness. He was used to taking care of himself and anyone else who crossed his path. The part of being the one in need didn't weigh well with him at all.

At the side of the bed, he released his death grip on her shoulder to fall, rolling to his back on the heaving mattress, one arm coming up to cover his eyes. Even with his eyes covered, he could still feel the room spinning. He inched a foot to the side of the bed and let it dangle.

"Do you want me to call the doctor?" she asked hesitantly.

"No. I just need to sleep it off." He rolled to his side, turning his back to her, shutting her out. "Why don't you go on home? You can take my truck. Joe'll drop me by later to pick it up."

Incensed that he thought she'd leave him like this, Marybeth gave his shoulder a yank, tugging him to his back. Ignoring the wince of pain the sudden movement brought him, she clamped her hands at her waist. "I'm *not* going home. I'm staying right here and taking care of you whether you like it or not."

She marched from the room and returned with the bottle of aspirin and a glass of water. Her lips pressed tight, she shook out two aspirin and extended her hand, palm up. Gunner's eyes met hers, dark with suppressed fury. Marybeth refused to let him intimidate her. She lifted her chin and glared right back. Finally he scraped the aspirin from her hand and popped them into his mouth. Grimacing, he propped himself up on one elbow and accepted the glass. He drank deeply, then held it out to her.

"Satisfied?" he asked as he collapsed back against the pillows.

"Almost." She set the glass on the floor by the bed, then propped her hip on the water bed's frame. "We need to talk."

"Now?"

"Yes, now."

"About what?"

"Our relationship."

He pressed a hand to his temple and rubbed, closing his eyes. "What about it?"

"Do you love me and Miranda?"

His eyes flipped open and he looked at her, the lines in his brow deepening. "Well, sure I do. I'd think you'd know that by now."

"I thought you did, too, until—well . . ." She took a deep breath and dropped her gaze to stare down at her hands in her lap. "While you were gone, I went into Laura's room." She lifted her gaze to his, her eyes filled with the doubts and confusion her visit to the room had raised. "Do you love us, Gunner? Or are you trying to keep Laura's memory alive through Miranda?"

Gunner jerked up to his elbows, the sudden movement making his head swim and pound. "Is that what you think?"

She met his furious glare with calmness. "I don't know what to think anymore." Unable to meet his gaze any longer, she dropped her eyes to her lap. "I don't understand why you restored Laura's room to the condition it was when she was alive, and I don't understand why you constantly put your life in danger. It's as if you feel you have to save everyone to make up for the loss of Phyllis and Laura." She found the courage to look at him again and to stretch a hand to touch his forearm. Her fingers circled and squeezed.

"I love you, Gunner, and Miranda loves you, as well. And we need you. But I have to know that you love us, too, for who we are and not some memory we can keep alive for you. And I have to know that you'll stop taking chances with your own life. I don't know what we'd do if anything happened to you."

She searched his face for any sign of understanding, but not once throughout her short speech and declaration of love did his eyes soften. Though she couldn't see it, there was a brick wall between them. One he'd erected and only he could tear down. His arm remained rigid and unyielding beneath her hand. Slowly she withdrew her hand and stood.

"Maybe you're right. Maybe I should go home." She turned and walked away, her chin dipped down to her chest. At the bedroom door she lifted her face to glance back. The sight of him stretched out on the bed, the bandage taped above his eye a glaring reminder of his close brush with death, pulled at her. The coldness in his eyes held her back.

"I'll call Joe and tell him your truck is at my house," she said softly, then closed the door behind her.

Ten

Marybeth whipped Gunner's truck onto her driveway and sent up a silent prayer of thanks when she saw no other cars parked there. Juanita wasn't home yet, nor were Helene and Miranda. She didn't think she could bear to see anyone just yet. She needed time to rest and think, to mentally and physically prepare herself for the explanations she knew she'd need to offer Miranda.

Gunner was gone.

A pain ripped through her chest and she bent to rest her forehead against the steering wheel of his truck. Had her suppositions been true? Had she and Miranda held so little value in his life he could let them go without so much as a backward glance? What was she to do with all these feelings she had for him? She didn't have an answer to that question but she was wise enough to know she couldn't make him love her.

And that was what she needed to accept. But how was she to explain his disappearance from their lives to Miranda when he didn't return to finish the playhouse?

At the disturbing thought, she lifted her head from the steering wheel and looked toward the backyard and the unfinished playhouse. Sunshine glinted off the silver heads of the roofing nails holding the black roofing paper in place. Today the shingles were to have been put on.

Pushing open the truck door, she crossed to the backyard and stopped in front of the playhouse's Dutch door. At her feet was the tiny front porch. She dipped her knees to kneel beside it, smoothing her hand across the three footprints impressed upon the concrete and the names scrawled beneath each. Gunner. Marybeth. Miranda. She remembered the day they'd performed the dedication and the thoughts she'd had. The circle of life complete.

Choking back tears, she rose and hurried for the house, turning her back on the memories as her breath hitched on the knots of emotion twisting in her chest.

"Marybeth?"

"Hmm?"

"Are you awake?"

"No."

Miranda giggled. "Well, wake up, sleepyhead!"

Marybeth rolled to her back and stretched. The tears shed earlier had dried on her cheeks, making them feel as if they'd been starched.

Rubbing her hands up and down her face, she forced her eyelids open. Squinting, she looked up at Miranda. Her daughter's cheeks were flushed, her eyes sunshine-bright, and not a smudge of makeup marred her face. A smile slowly built on Marybeth's face. Oh, how she loved this little girl of hers. "Hi, Princess."

"Hi." Miranda dropped down onto the side of the bed. "Mamere just left. She told Juanita and me to let you sleep since you'd obviously had a long night." She giggled and flipped to lie down beside her mother. "But while Juanita was unpacking, I snuck back here so I could see if you were awake."

Marybeth gathered Miranda in her arms and squeezed, needing to feel the warmth and comfort of her daughter's body close to hers. "You're a scamp."

"I know." She giggled again and cuddled closer to Marybeth. "But I wanted to ask you when Gunner was coming to put the roof on the playhouse."

Marybeth brushed Miranda's bangs away from her face and placed a kiss on her forehead. "I'm not sure, sweetheart."

Frowning, Miranda glanced up. "Is he working?"

"No." Marybeth sighed. "He was hurt last night at a fire. When I left him, he was going to sleep. We better not count on seeing him today."

"Was he hurt badly?"

"No. Nothing serious."

"Then when's he coming back?"

Marybeth caught the back of Miranda's neck in her hand and pulled her face to her neck. "I don't know, sweetheart. I just don't know."

Miranda sat at Marybeth's vanity with bottles, tubes, jars and brushes scattered at her fingertips. She clamped her lips around a tissue, blotting the fiery red lipstick, and leaving a perfect impression of her lips on the tissue's whiteness. Angling her head to one side, she puckered her mouth and studied the effect in the mirror.

Perfect, she decided, liking the three shades of color on her eyelids and the peach blush on her cheeks as well as the color on her lips. Standing, she adjusted the brass belt at her waist, thinking sometimes adults could be so stupid. "Okay, Marybeth," she murmured to her reflection. "I've had it with you and Gunner. If y'all can't work this thing out between you, then I guess it's up to me."

Firming her lips, she turned, tottering slightly in her mother's heels, and headed for the front of the house. As she approached her mother's office, she slowed her step and tiptoed to the door. She placed her ear against the cool wood. The sound of the typewriter, muffled but distinct, vibrated against her cheek and ear.

Knowing Juanita was in her room, enjoying her afternoon siesta, Miranda hurried on to the kitchen, smiling her satisfaction that all the parts of her plan were falling into place. After quietly removing the portable phone from it's base on the kitchen counter, she tiptoed to the back door, eased it open and slipped outside, closing the door softly behind her.

On the back porch, she stopped, filling her lungs with a deep breath. "Ready or not," she whispered to the blue sky above, "here I come." Smiling, she skipped down the steps.

Needing a break, Marybeth rose and stretched, arching her back and twining her hands high above her head. Though she'd been sitting at her desk all morning, she knew she hadn't accomplished nearly as much on the articles as she should. She dropped her hands to her sides on a weary sigh.

And it was Gunner's fault. More than a week had passed without a word from him. It was one thing for him to cut her out of his life, and quite another for him to do the same to Miranda. Miranda was only a child and she didn't understand relationships. She just knew she loved Gunner and that for some reason, he wasn't interested in her anymore.

Marybeth had tried her darnedest to explain to Miranda that Gunner's disappearance had nothing to do with her. But Marybeth couldn't help wondering if her daughter really understood the complexity of it all. Her mood over the past week suggested she felt responsible somehow. She'd been quieter than usual, more subdued. Nothing seemed to interest her. Except the playhouse. She'd sit on the back doorstep and stare at it for hours on end, her chin propped in her hand.

Shaking her head at the worries that nagged at her, Marybeth crossed the office and pulled open the door. A glance at her watch told her Juanita would be resting in her room and Miranda watching television. It was an arrangement the two had made when Miranda outgrew the need for an afternoon nap. From one to three every afternoon, Juanita would rest in her room and Miranda would watch television. At three, Miranda was assured Juanita's undivided attention for two hours before the housekeeper prepared dinner.

Knowing this, Marybeth headed for the den. "Miranda?" she called as entered the room. The television was on and cartoon characters flipped across the screen in a flurry of color. Marybeth strode to the back of the couch and peeked over, expecting to see Miranda curled there, her eyes glued on the set. But no Miranda.

Frowning, Marybeth turned and headed for the bedroom wing of the house. A glance in Miranda's room proved she wasn't there, either, and Marybeth moved on to her room and the dressing area beyond. One panel of her closet's mirrored door was slid back and clothes were piled on the floor and a mishmash of shoes lay jumbled about.

At her vanity, her gaze froze and her eyes widened. The drawer gaped open, its contents strewn across the vanity's marble top. "Oh no," she moaned in dismay.

"Flip the channel to seven for a minute."

Gunner turned to frown at Joe, his hand tightening defensively around the remote control. "My soap is on."

"So?" When Gunner didn't move, Joe rolled his eyes. "That dark-haired woman is going to fight with her boyfriend and go crying home to her mother. That old couple is going to take in another orphan, only to have the kid's mother show up and cause havoc in their lives. And that other dame is going to have a relapse and get roaring drunk. Now," he said, leaning to snatch the control from Gunner's hand, "you know everything that's going to happen. So let's watch the interview with Arnold Schwarzenegger."

Joe's move was so smooth, Gunner didn't realize he'd lost the control until he heard the sound change from one channel to the next. With a last glare at Joe, he crossed his arms over his chest and sank back against the sofa cushions to stare at the screen. What met his eye made his heart slam against his chest. Marybeth stood in a mock kitchen behind a center island, stirring and laughing as she chatted with the show's host.

The man dipped his head over the pan and sniffed. "I think I just gained ten pounds."

Marybeth laughed and lifted the spoon from the pan, angling it a bit and letting the creamy sauce spill over the side for a better camera shot. "No you won't," she said, with a firm shake of her head. "That's the beauty of this recipe. Low fat, low salt, but without losing the flavor of great chicken enchiladas."

The host tipped his head, to run his gaze down Marybeth's length. "I know that you experiment a lot with recipes, which surely means you must do a lot of tasting. How do you stay so slim?"

Gunner didn't hear Marybeth's reply. He was too damn mad. Blood pulsed in his ears, creating a roar that blotted out all other sound. The guy had the nerve, cozying up to Marybeth like that, practically undressing her with his eyes. He watched Marybeth laugh and artfully sidestep the man's attention. The sight of her with another man sickened him. He lurched to his feet and turned his back on the set.

Joe glanced up. "Where're you going?"

"Nowhere." Gunner strode to the kitchen, to escape the sight of Marybeth. He didn't want to look at her. He didn't want or need the reminder. Her image haunted him daily. At the kitchen sink, he twisted on the faucet and pushed a glass under the flow of water. Tipping back his head, he drank long and deeply, wetting his dry throat and cooling his temper.

After draining the glass, he dropped his wrists to the sink's edge and his forehead to his biceps. God, how he missed her. Not a day went by that he didn't pick up the phone to call her or head his truck in the direction of her house. But before he could carry out either one of his attempts at reconciliation, he'd remember her accusations, her doubts.

But dammit, she just didn't understand. He'd never confused Miranda with Laura. The kid had won his heart from the first moment he'd set eyes on her. His love for Marybeth had been a little slower in growing. In fact he couldn't put his finger on the precise moment he'd realized the depth of his feelings for her. But he loved them both, to him it was as simple as that.

The alarm sounded and he snapped up his head. He could see Joe barreling toward the kitchen.

When he reached the doorway, he leaned his head through, gripping either side of the facing. The worry knotting his brow concerned Gunner. His words scared the hell out of him.

"Nine-one-one—407 Maple Drive," Joe said, before pushing away from the door.

"Miranda," Gunner murmured. He shoved the glass to the kitchen counter and took off at a run.

The doorbell sounded just as Marybeth stepped from her room. Anxious to find Miranda, she ignored it, intent on continuing her search. The pounding that followed made her stop and she glanced back down the hallway. *What in the world?* she wondered, puzzled by the urgency of whomever stood on the opposite side. She hurried back down the hall.

Twisting the door's handle, she pulled it wide. She fell back a step, her hand going to her throat. Gunner stood in front of her and, parked in the driveway, the fire truck's flashing lights whirled. Joe was running across the front lawn. A sense of déjà vu swept over her.

"Miranda," she murmured as fear tightened her chest. Spinning away, she charged for the kitchen, then whirled only to slam into Gunner's chest.

He caught her arms in his hands, steadying her. "Where is she?"

Marybeth fought to control the tremble in her voice. "I don't know. I was looking for her when you came."

"Could she be hiding?"

"Not in the house. I've looked everywhere."

Their eyes met and knowledge dawned. "The playhouse," they said at the same moment.

They both took off at a run, their shoulders bumping as they tried to pass through the kitchen doorway at the same time. Frustrated, Marybeth squeezed past him and hurried to the back door. Twisting it open, she flew down the steps, with Gunner a half step behind her.

At the playhouse, she paused, catching her breath. Beyond the Dutch door she could hear Miranda singing a lullaby.

"Hush little baby, don't you cry..."

Her voice was soft and sweet, the words achingly familiar. Tom had sung the song to Miranda almost daily from the time she'd been born until the day he'd died.

Swallowing hard to keep the tears at bay, Marybeth eased open the door and stepped inside. Miranda sat in Laura's rocker, crooning the lyrics of the song to a baby doll clutched at her chest. "...Daddy's going to buy you a diamond ring. If that diamond ring don't—"

"Miranda."

Miranda snapped her head around to look at Marybeth. She stared a moment then lifted her gaze higher, looking above and beyond Marybeth. Tears budded in her eyes and she lowered her gaze. Giving the rocker a nudge with the toe of a high-heeled shoe, she set it in motion. She gathered the baby tighter in her arms, humming the lullaby.

Without looking, Marybeth knew Gunner stood behind her and it was the sight of him that had drawn Miranda's tears. She also knew Miranda had dialed 9-1-1 to get Gunner to the house. And she couldn't let her get away with that.

"Miranda," she said, firming the quiver from her voice. "Did you dial 9-1-1?"

The rocker stilled, but Miranda didn't look up. "Yes."

"Why?"

"Gunner said if I ever needed him, I could call."

"I don't think he meant for you to dial 9-1-1. There are other numbers available for personal calls—9-1-1 is strictly for emergencies."

"This is an emergency."

"What emer—"

Gunner stepped up beside Marybeth and laid his hand on her arm, shushing her. She looked up at him, her eyes filled with a pain that matched that grabbing at his chest.

"Let me talk to her," he said in a low voice, nodding his head toward the door. "Why don't you go inside and tell Joe to send everyone home?"

Marybeth opened her mouth to argue the point, then closed it again, pressing her lips tightly together. She knew it was best to let Gunner talk to Miranda. After all, he was the one behind her discontent.

When the door closed behind Marybeth, Gunner crossed to Miranda and dropped down on one knee. "What did you want to talk to me about, Princess?"

Her lower lip quivered as she tipped her face to his. "Don't you love us anymore?"

The question tore at his heart. He reached out and took her hand in his, squeezing it in reassurance. "Sure I do."

"But you don't ever come over anymore and you haven't finished my playhouse."

Sighing, Gunner bowed his head to stare at the floor. How could he explain to this precious little girl all that stood behind his absence? Especially since he didn't really understand it all himself? Sucking in a deep breath, he blew it out, frustration puffing his cheeks and lips behind the force of air. "Your mother and I had a little misunderstanding," he said slowly.

"About what?"

Gunner shifted uncomfortably. His experience with kids was limited and what little he had was years old. He didn't know how best to explain the misunderstanding, but the openness and honesty in Miranda's questions demanded an open and honest response from him, as well. "Your mother seems to think I've confused you and Laura in my mind and that I'm just using you to keep Laura's memory alive." He watched her face, needing to measure her reaction, her level of understanding. "Do you feel that way, too?"

Miranda's brow knitted, but she responded without hesitation. "No, I know you love me and Laura, too."

Gunner's shoulders sagged in relief. "I'm glad you understand that, Princess." He squeezed her hand again. "'Cause I do love you and Laura, but not as the same person or even in the same way."

Miranda dropped her one-handed grip on the baby doll to throw her arms around Gunner's neck. "I love you, too, Gunner," she whispered against his ear. She leaned back to look up at him. "Does this mean you'll come back and see me and work on my playhouse again?"

"Before I promise anything, I better go have a talk with your mother." He stood, catching her hands in his. "But no matter what, I'll always love you, Miranda. Remember that, okay?"

She returned the smile, her face beaming. "Okay."

He turned and headed for the door, stooping to duck through the opening.

"Gunner?"

He glanced back. "What?"

Miranda held up her fist, her thumb pointing up. "Good luck."

Chuckling, he shook his head as he turned away. "Thanks. I have a feeling I'm going to need it."

Joe sat at the bar, hugging his coffee cup between his hands, savoring the smell of the exotic blend of beans. Marybeth paced in front of him, wringing her hands at her waist.

"How can I be sure?" she asked, turning a pleading look to Joe.

"You can't. You've just got to trust him."

Marybeth dropped her hands to her sides, her shoulders sagging helplessly. "If it were just me, I wouldn't care. I know I can handle whatever happens. But Miranda is so fragile. She's only just now coming to terms with the loss of her father."

"Give the kid some credit. She's a lot stronger than you think."

"You don't understand. Miranda worships Gunner. To her, he is—"

The back door swung open behind her, and Marybeth whirled just as Gunner stepped into the kitchen. He paused, looking from one to the other. A frown gathered on his forehead and he dropped his gaze as he turned to close the door behind him.

Joe was on his feet in a heartbeat, his burst of motion and his forced smile making him look as guilty as hell. "Ready to go, Chief?"

"Not quite. But you can. I'm taking the afternoon off."

Marybeth's mouth dropped open in surprise and she flicked her gaze to Joe. His expression was a mirror image of her own. And no wonder. Joe knew better than she that Gunner Keith hadn't taken a day off from the fire station in the ten years he'd worked there.

Gunner frowned at Joe. "You *can* handle things at the station, can't you?"

"Well, sure, Chief, but…" Joe grinned and slapped his hat on his head. "Never mind. Enjoy yourself," he said, giving Marybeth a wink. The swinging door flapped twice, exposing a view of his retreating back before settling back on its hinges. Suddenly it was just Marybeth and Gunner in the room. The silence was deafening.

Uncomfortable with it, she crossed to the coffeepot. "Would you like a cup?" she asked.

Gunner levered a hip onto a bar stool. "Yeah, I would."

She pushed the cup in front of him, then leaned to slide the sugar bowl within his reach. He acknowledged the gesture with a tip of his head as he leveled a heaping spoon of sugar in his cup. Without looking at her, he patted the stool next to him. "Why don't you join me?"

Marybeth didn't know what was coming and wasn't sure she wanted to know. Hesitantly she took the seat.

Gunner sipped at the coffee, then set the cup back on the bar. "I talked with Miranda."

"Did she tell you why she called?"

"Yeah. She said she thought I didn't love her anymore because I didn't come see her and because I haven't finished her playhouse. By dialing 9-1-1, she hoped to get things straight between us. I told her the reason for my absence was that you and I had had a little misunderstanding."

Marybeth eyed him warily. "You did?"

"Yeah." He frowned at his coffee as he turned the cup within the circle of his hands. "I've done a lot of thinking since I saw you last. Some of the things you said that morning made sense, but some of it was just plain crap." He twisted around on his bar stool and caught the back of her chair, swiveling it until their knees bumped. His eyes were dark with intensity as he met her gaze. "The first room I remodeled after the fire was Laura's room. I really can't tell you why. Maybe it was out of guilt. Or maybe it was because every time I walked past her room, I saw her lying in that bed the way I'd found her. Whatever the reason, I did what I did to blot out the reminders of that night, not to keep her memory alive."

Holding her gaze with his, he caught her hands. "But you've got to believe me, Marybeth, when I tell you I never confused Laura and Miranda. That little girl of yours captured my heart that first morning when I saw her standing in the kitchen dressed like some cheap floozy.'' He squeezed her hands within his, willing her to understand how the reminders of the fire had haunted him until one by one he'd removed them, and to make her believe him when he said he truly cared for Miranda and not the memory of Laura.

Tears welled in Marybeth's eyes as she watched the emotions work across Gunner's face. She did believe him. How could she do otherwise when he was opening up his heart and baring his soul this way?

His grip tightened around her fingers. "And I love you, Marybeth. That morning when you questioned my feelings for you and Miranda—'' At the memory, he dropped his gaze to his knees, unable to finish the statement. His lips firmed to a thin line and the muscles worked in his jaw. "Well, I can't tell you how badly that hurt." He tipped his head to look at her again. "I know I've never said it before. I'm not a man who's good with pretty words." A smile tugged at one corner of his mouth. "Joe's the one with all the charm." His smile faded, his expression once again serious. "But surely you must know how much I love you. Please tell me you do?''

"Oh, Gunner, I do." She curled her fingers around his broad palm, seeking his understanding as well. "But what about your job? The chances you take...I don't know if Miranda or I could survive losing you."

Gunner shook his head and dropped his gaze to his knees once again. "That's the one thing you said that morning that wasn't crap." His shoulders rose and fell in a weary sigh. He lifted his face to look her square in the eye. "I realize now I've been obsessive about my

job. Partly because I didn't have anything else to focus on. Without Laura and Phyllis to care for, I just
naturally put all my time and energy into my work. I
think you were right, too, when you said I was trying
to absolve myself of guilt. I'll never know if I could
have saved them that night if I'd been home. As a result, every time an alarm sounds, I go. After ten years,
the response is automatic. I honestly feel that if I don't
go, the outcome might in some way be different. I
know that's not healthy for me or anyone else whose
life touches mine.''

The ball of his thumbs moved in the curve of her
hand. ''I've lived with the guilt a long time, Marybeth. I can't promise I can change overnight. But it'd
help if you were there to remind me I have a future and
not just a past.''

She swallowed hard, trying to find her voice, not
wanting to read anything into his words. ''Gunner,
what are you saying?''

''I guess I'm asking you to marry me. I'm not sure
what kind of husband or father I'll make, but you
have my promise I'll work hard at being the best at
both.''

''Oh, Gunner.'' The tears brimming in her eyes
slipped to spill down her cheeks. She jerked her hands
free to scrape the tears from her cheeks, then instead
threw them around his neck. She hugged him to her.
''Yes, I'll marry you. And I know without a doubt
you'll be the best husband and father in the world.''

They rocked back and forth, locked in each other's
arms. But Marybeth soon discovered being in his arms
simply wasn't enough. She had to taste him, to make
that unified link. She found his lips and filled his

mouth with the warmth of a contented sigh. "I love you so much, Gunner," she whispered against his lips.

His arms tightened protectively around her, forcing her closer to his chest and deeper between his spread knees. "I love you, too, Marybeth," he whispered in return before taking her mouth in a breathtaking kiss.

Through the webs of passion humming around her, Marybeth heard the back door ease open.

"Mom?"

Marybeth and Gunner froze at the same instant, their lips still locked. They pushed back to stare into each other's face, then in unison turned toward the door. Miranda stood in the doorway, her cheeks streaked with mascara from the tears she'd shed earlier.

Marybeth slipped from the stool, her trembling fingers finding their way to her mouth. She crossed the room as if in a daze. "Miranda, you called me Mom."

Miranda wrinkled her nose. "So?"

"Honey, you haven't called me Mom in—oh, never mind," she said, tears clotting her throat, making speaking impossible. She dropped to her knees and pulled Miranda to her breasts.

Gunner knelt beside them, catching them both in the circle of his arms. Miranda giggled as she squirmed to slip an arm around first Marybeth's neck, then Gunner's.

"We're like a real family," she said, looking from one to the other.

Smoothing the hair back from her daughter's face, Marybeth tucked it behind Miranda's ear. "Would you like that, Princess?"

"Would Gunner live here with us?"

Marybeth glanced over the top of Miranda's head to look at Gunner. The smile they shared was full of the love they felt for each other. "Either here or at his farm. We haven't discussed that yet."

Miranda drew back a step and frowned. "But what about my playhouse?"

Gunner tossed back his head and laughed. Out of the mouths of babes, he thought. "No matter where we live, Princess, I promise you'll always have your playhouse."

Remembering how Gunner had placed Laura's playhouse over her grave, Miranda curled her fingers around his neck. "Just like Laura," she said on a sigh.

Knowing he could never love the kid any more than he did at that very moment, Gunner dipped his forehead to touch hers. "Yes, just like Laura."

*   *   *   *   *

MYSTERY MATES!

Six sexy Bachelors explosively pair with six sultry Bachelorettes to find the Valentine's surprise of a lifetime.

Get to know the mysterious men who breeze into the lives of these unsuspecting women. Slowly uncover—as the heroines themselves must do—the missing pieces of the puzzle that add up to hot, *hot* heroes! You begin by knowing nothing about these enigmatic men, but soon you'll know *everything*. . . .

Heat up your winter with:

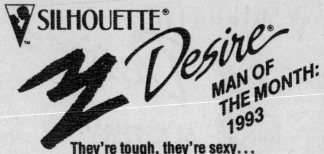

For all those readers who've been looking for something a little bit different, a little bit spooky, let Silhouette Books take you on a journey to the dark side of love with

If you like your romance mixed with a hint of danger, a taste of something eerie and wild, you'll love Shadows. This new line will send a shiver down your spine and make your heart beat faster. It's full of romance and more—and some of your favorite authors will be featured right from the start. Look for our four launch titles wherever books are sold, because you won't want to miss a single one.

THE LAST CAVALIER—Heather Graham Pozzessere
WHO IS DEBORAH?—Elise Title
STRANGER IN THE MIST—Lee Karr
SWAMP SECRETS—Carla Cassidy

After that, look for two books every month, and prepare to tremble with fear—and passion.

SILHOUETTE SHADOWS, coming your way in March.

SHAD1

Take 4 bestselling love stories FREE

Plus get a FREE surprise gift!

Special Limited-time Offer

Mail to Silhouette Reader Service™

3010 Walden Avenue
P.O. Box 1867
Buffalo, N.Y. 14269-1867

YES! Please send me 4 free Silhouette Desire® novels and my free surprise gift. Then send me 6 brand-new novels every month, which I will receive months before they appear in bookstores. Bill me at the low price of $2.24* each plus 25¢ delivery and applicable sales tax, if any.* I understand that accepting the books and gift places me under no obligation ever to buy any books. I can always return a shipment and cancel at any time. Even if I never buy another book from Silhouette, the 4 free books and the surprise gift are mine to keep forever.

225 BPA AJCJ

Name	(PLEASE PRINT)	
Address		Apt No.
City	State	Zip

UDES-93   ©1990 Harlequin Enterprises Limited

**Silhouette Books
is proud to present
our best authors,
their best books...
and the best in
your reading pleasure!**

Throughout 1993, look for exciting books
by these top names in contemporary
romance:

CATHERINE COULTER—
Aftershocks in February

FERN MICHAELS—
Whisper My Name in March

DIANA PALMER—
Heather's Song in March

ELIZABETH LOWELL—
Love Song for a Raven in April

SANDRA BROWN
(previously published under
the pseudonym Erin St. Claire)—
Led Astray in April

LINDA HOWARD—
All That Glitters in May

When it comes to passion,
we wrote the book.

Silhouette®